Moscow Calling

A novel by

Neal Hardin

ISBN 9781983133848

To my Uncle Dave and Aunt Jackie.

Acknowledgement

To, my friend, Peter Williams for his advice, guidance and suggestions.

Chapter 1

Friday 2nd October 2015, London

The auctioneer was a bespectacled man in a crushed velvet suit of cobalt blue. A white handkerchief was lodged in the breast pocket of his jacket. He had the air of a debonair soul with his bouffant hair and a tan that was probably made on a sunbed in a local solarium. He had a kind of retro cool befitting a villain in a James Bond movie. Before he got down to the next item on the list of articles for sale, he took the water filled glass on the podium and put the rim to his lips. He took a sip of the liquid, then his eyes went onto the people in the audience before him.

"Ladies and gentlemen," he said. "We now come to lot number eighteen of today's auction, page number twenty-four in your brochure. A pair of exquisite, hand-crafted eggs from the House of Faberge. Circa eighteen-ninety, with gold and silver leaf trim and hand-crafted inlay of the highest quality, befitting such a distinguished house." His accent was very la-di-da.

He paused for a moment to let his words soak in and to let the members of the audience put their eyes on a live camera shot of the eggs, projected onto a large screen on the back wall. His words were accompanied by a rustle of the glossy pages of brochures being turned, then a buzz of chat coming from the mouths of the four hundred people in the audience. Faberge eggs certainly got the attention of the gathering, for they were without doubt two of the most beautiful artefacts to be auctioned today. The man in the crushed velvet suit took the glass for a second time and had another sip of liquid. It might be the last chance he would have to wet his tonsils before the auction got underway. He placed the glass on the lectern, then raised his eyes again to the audience. The man in the long khaki coat standing aside the beautiful objects took a step back. The neon figures in the list of currencies displayed in the panel aside the screen were all set at zero. There were several currencies: US dollars, Japanese Yen, Chinese Yuan, and Russian Roubles to name just four, along with British pounds sterling.

"I want to start the bidding for these lovely items at two hundred and fifty thousand pounds," the auctioneer said in his posh accent. As he said those words, as if by magic, the numbers in the panel by the currencies began to rev up to the equivalent of two hundred and fifty thousand pounds sterling.

Dimitri Priskin was sitting at the back of the audience, on the eightieth row of twenty. He put his mobile phone to his mouth. "The eggs are about to be bid for," he said into the speaker. His accent was quintessentially metropolitan London with an eastern European edge. The words were delivered in one hundred percent Russian.

"Do I have two hundred and sixty thousand pounds?" the auctioneer asked. Someone at the front of the audience raised a paddle with the number, 'two-seven-eight' on it.

"Thank you," said the auctioneer. "Do I have two hundred and seventy thousand pounds?" he asked. Another paddle with another number, this time in the middle of the audience, on the left-hand side was raised high.

The man in the fancy Dan suit looked around the room. "Two hundred and eighty thousand pounds?" he asked.

Dimitri Priskin raised the paddle in his hand. His number was, 'two-eight-five'.

As the bids went up, the figures in the panel on the screen increased and the neon numbers glowed bright against the dark background.

The auctioneer looked in Priskin's direction. "Thank you," he said. "The bid is at two hundred and eighty thousand pounds. Do I have two hundred and ninety thousand pounds?" he asked.

The paddle of the bidder at the front of the audience was raised. He was back in the hunt. Once again, the auctioneer acknowledged the bid.

"The bid is at two hundred and ninety thousand. Do I have three hundred thousand pounds?"

Someone, a new bidder, on the right-hand side of the audience, about halfway down the rows raised a paddle with the number, 'two-nine-six' on it. The bidding had reached three hundred thousand in less than one minute. As the bids came in, Dimitri

Priskin continued to speak into his telephone to update the listener on the other end of the line.

The bidding continued unabated. It went from three hundred thousand to three hundred and forty thousand in no time. The atmosphere in the room was white hot. You could cut the tension with a sharp blade. There was an almost impenetrable hiss of subdued chit-chat coming from the audience. The bidding for these two beautiful works of art might go on for some time.

The bidding soon hit four hundred thousand pounds. Three bidders were still in the hunt. The bidder at the front with paddle number, 'two-seven-eight' was still in the game. The bidder on the right-hand side with paddle number, 'two-nine-six' was keeping up with the pace. The third bidder was Dimitri Priskin.

Minutes passed. There was a glint of perspiration on the auctioneer's forehead. His carefully crafted bouffant reflected the light as if it was coated with lacquer. His voice was still strong and clear, and he kept the bidding going at a crisp even canter to ensure the pace didn't slacken. The bidding soon reached 38,000,000 Russian roubles, 664,000 US Dollars. 73,000,000 Japanese Yen. 500,000 British pounds sterling. There were still three players in the fray. Dimitri Priskin and the other two bidders who steadfastly refused to give in.

The bid was with Priskin. "Do I have five hundred and ten thousand pounds?" asked the auctioneer. He glanced down to the bidder at the front of the room, then to the other one to his left.

The chap to Priskin's right lifted his paddle aloft. The auctioneer's eyes went to the bidder at the front of the room. "The bid is five hundred and ten thousand pounds. Do I have five hundred and twenty thousand?" he asked.

The paddle from the bidder at the front did not rise. The whispers from the audience increased. One of the bidders had pulled out. The camera zoomed in on the artefacts glinting in the beam aimed at them. The turquoise shell and intricate gold and silver thread gleamed and sparkled. The auctioneer's eyes went to Priskin.

"Do I have five hundred and twenty thousand pounds?" he asked.

Priskin lifted his paddle high once again. The auctioneer's eyes went from him to his left, Priskin's right. Perhaps the end game had been reached.

"The bid is against you," said the auctioneer, bowing his head slightly to talk into the microphone attached to the lapel of his blue crushed velvet jacket.

The bidder raised his paddle, once again. The ball was back in Priskin court at thirty-nine million roubles. If he went to five hundred and thirty thousand pounds that would be over forty million Russian roubles.

"It's at forty million," Priskin said into his phone.

"Take it to forty-six million," said the voice on the other end of the line.

Priskin raised his paddle for the umpteenth time in the past five minutes. He glanced over to his right to try and lay his eyes on the other bidder. From what he could see from this angle, the bidder was a grey-haired hirsute man in his mid-forties. He was wearing a light jacket. The collar of his shirt was visible above the collar of the jacket. He had dark shades over his eyes. He may have been British, but as he hadn't said a word it was impossible to tell. Most of the people around Priskin were British, after all this was an auction house in central London. You couldn't get more central London than Bond Street if you tried.

The auctioneer lifted his right hand, cupped his fingers, and gestured in the direction of the chap in the light jacket. "The bid is at five hundred and thirty thousand pounds. It's against you Sir. Do I hear five hundred and forty thousand pounds?" he asked.

Once again, the man raised the paddle with the numbers 'two-nine-six' in black bold numbers against a white background. The whispers in the room increased three-fold. The numbers in the panel changed in the flick of an eyelid. Five hundred and forty thousand pounds was the equivalent of 41,396,400 Russian roubles. The ball was back in Dimitri Priskin's court. He raised the paddle again.

The other bidder did likewise. The bidding had reached five hundred and sixty thousand pounds. Priskin advised the person on the other end of the line that the sum was now nearly forty-three million roubles.

"Is the other bidder going to pull out?" the man on the other end of the line asked.

"*это, похоже, не так*". *It doesn't appear to be the case,* said Priskin.

"*Пусть у него есть это.*" Let *him have them,* said the voice, *then,* "*узнайте, кто он.*" *Find out who the other bidder is,* instructed the voice in a piqued tone.

"The bid is five hundred and sixty thousand pounds," said the auctioneer addressing not only Priskin, but the audience.

A hundred pairs of eyes went in Priskin's direction. He smiled, then sighed, shook his head in resignation and placed the paddle in his lap. The end-game had been reached.

The auctioneer raised his head. "The bid is at five hundred and sixty thousand pounds. Are there any more bidders?" His eyes went around the room from one side to the other, from back to front. "Any more bidders?" he asked again. He had the gavel in his right hand. Ready to bring it down. "Are we all done? At five hundred and sixty thousand pounds…" He raised his hand. His eyes went around the room for the final time. "Are we all done?" he asked again.

He dropped his hand and the head of the gavel made a sharp clap on the base of a knocker. "Yours Sir. For five hundred and sixty thousand pounds," he said addressing the man to Priskin's right.

Priskin immediately turned his phone off and slipped it into his jacket pocket. He didn't hang about. He rose from his seat, moved out of the row, stepped down the aisle, then out of the room. All without making eye contact with the man who had just denied his boss the two exquisite Faberge eggs.

Chapter 2

On leaving the auction house, Priskin walked the short distance towards Piccadilly at the Green Park end of the busy thoroughfare. Once on Piccadilly, he stepped onto the edge of the road and raised his hand to stop a passing black cab which had its 'for hire' sign illuminated. Despite living in London for the past fourteen years Priskin very rarely drove in central London, choosing instead to use taxis as his preferred method of getting around the city.

At five-thirty, the late-afternoon Friday traffic was heavy. As were the pavements with office workers heading home for the weekend. The driver took him to the place he had requested and stopped along Knightsbridge adjacent to a pair of heavy iron gates that blocked off a private road on the western edge of the thoroughfare, close to Hyde Park. Priskin got out of the cab and paid the driver.

Beyond the gate was a cobbled road that was lined with elegant Georgian style mansions. The area was peppered with CCTV cameras and had its own private security, independent of the Met police. After all some very wealthy and prominent people lived in the parade of exclusive homes.

Yuri Asamovich, Dimitri Priskin's boss, resided in a six-bedroom house that had once belonged to the Shah of Iran, then an American tycoon before Asamovich purchased it for fifteen million pounds when he came to London in 2002. Asamovich had gotten the bargain of a lifetime and he knew it.

The uniformed security guard, sitting in the box at the other side of the fence, recognised Priskin from the hundreds of times he had visited his boss. The man gave him a nod of his head, then he opened the pedestrian gate in the fence and allowed him through the barrier. "Good evening," he said as Priskin stepped through the gate, then closed it behind him with a solid clatter.

"Good evening," replied Priskin. He walked along the path at the side of the cobbled road. The homes of the occupants, along Caradon Walk, Knightsbridge, where set behind a continuous ten-feet high black iron rail fence then lawns of grass and shrub filled gardens. As he went along the path Priskin looked skyward. The insipid light of the day was fading fast at five-forty in the afternoon. The sky was fringed with a pink and orange backdrop so there was a beautiful light that gave the city a colourful glow.

Dimitri Priskin was Russian, through and through, though he did have British blood in his veins. His mother was British. Dimitri Priskin had dual Russian-British nationality. Thinking about his mother reminded him that he needed to take a trip along the M4 to the Clifton Village area of Bristol where she resided, especially before the autumn set in and it became too dark and too gloomy to drive there and back in a day. He hated driving in the dark.

Priskin ventured along the path with his hands deep in his pockets and his shoulders hunched. The programme he had taken from the desk when he entered the auction house was wedged inside a jacket pocket. Yuri Asamovich wouldn't be pleased that he had been out-bid for the two Faberge eggs. He had his heart set on owning them and displaying them in a cabinet along with several other items like the fine Chinese porcelain and the Ming vases he collected. He wouldn't be pleased, far from it. He would be resentful that someone had the temerity to bid more than him for two prized artefacts from his homeland. He would want to know who the bidder was and where he or she came from so he could hold something against them. How come this person had the money to pay £560,000 for the eggs? He would struggle to grasp the reality that someone wanted to own them more than he did and had the financial muscle to ensure it happened.

On reaching the gate to Asamovich's property, Priskin paused to straighten his tie. Then he pressed the button in the aluminium face of the communication box and waited for a reply. The façade of the house loomed high across the lawn and the pebble drive-way at the front. The water feature in the garden, a stone plinth atop a column, spouted a single jet of water into the air for a couple of feet before it fell back into the surrounding bowl. The starlings that would sit on the rim during the summer months were nowhere to be seen. The stone block on the front elevation shaded the area by the central doorway. The pastel blinds in the windows on all three floors were down. There was a trace of light in a ground floor

15

window to the right of the doorway and in the window on the left-hand side on the first floor. The Russian flag attached to the flag pole by the front door was hanging limp like a damp rag. The red and the blue colours were hardly visible in the dim twilight.

Asamovich didn't like to use telephones. He preferred face-to-face meetings in the comfort of his home and not in range of cameras with zoom lenses. He didn't trust the British Intelligence Service not to eavesdrop on his private conversations. He once said that his house was bugged, so for peace of mind he had a security expert flown in from Russia to carry out a full survey of the house. The man found nothing, but it still bugged him. As a friend of Vladimir Putin and a host of top Russian government officials he had to be careful. The British, the Americans, the French or whoever were keen to hear any snippets of information regarding Russians and their interests around the globe. They would get the information any way they could.

Priskin looked back at the shiny heads of the cobbled stones reflecting the streetlights. He could hear the hum of traffic on Knightsbridge. It was a few seconds before his call was answered by a rather curt 'yes' in Russian. It was Asamovich's housekeeper, a rather nice genial lady called Mrs. Andropov.

"It's Dimitri Priskin," he replied in Russian. From this point onward until he left the house all conversation would be in Russian. A language he had learned from the moment he could hear and decipher words whilst sitting on his father's knee in their apartment on the eighth floor of a block overlooking Gorky Park.

There was a 'buzz' as the bolt slid open. He opened the gate, closed it behind him then stepped along the path across the lawn and onto the crunchy pebbles in front of the main entrance. The shrub in the earthenware pot in the doorway looked as if it was flagging. The autumn had taken some of the leaves.

He opened the front door and stepped into the warmth of the rotunda shaped reception room. A black carpeted curved staircase hugged the wall on its way up to the first floor. Alternative black and white tiles covered the floor. The grim faces of the portraits in the picture frames on the staircase wall looked down with disapproving glares and expressions of angst and displeasure. Priskin didn't like the house. It gave him goosepimples every time he stepped through the front door. It was cold and unwelcoming. Like the location of a recurring nightmare that wouldn't go away.

A single black door in the wall opened and Yuri Asamovich emerged. He looked as glum and as unwelcoming as the faces in the portraits. Asamovich was a short man in his mid-sixties with a paunch and a slightly unbalanced physique. One leg appeared to be shorter than the other. He had a limp which he blamed on an injury sustained whilst out hunting wild boar in his youth. He had a stout barrel chest beneath the open neck salmon-pink shirt he was wearing under a dark jacket. His trousers were light and baggy.

Yuri Asamovich was a formidable man. He had an ice-like temperament and a no-nonsense approach to life and his business dealings. He eyed Priskin with his familiar icy stare. He paused to take a spectacles case from out of a jacket pocket, open it and extract a pair of reading glasses which he fitted over his eyes. His hair, which was thinning, but naturally black was swept over the crown of his head. His flesh was tanned and shiny. A visit to a plastic surgeon had given him a tight, wrinkle-free face for someone who would be sixty-seven-years-of-age in a few weeks from now.

"Who bought the eggs?" he asked in Russian. His words bounced in the circular space.

"Another bidder went over the limit you set," said Priskin.

"I know that. Who is he?" Asamovich asked.

"I don't know. I've never seen him before in my life."

"Find out," said Asamovich. "And make him an offer he can't refuse," he added.

Priskin didn't reply. This was something he hadn't heard before, either in jest or in genuine seriousness. Jest was something he didn't do too often. "Find him. Ask him if he wants to reconsider his bid. Tell him you'll make him an offer of what he paid. I want those eggs. They belong in a Russian home," he said in his Moscow accent. He had a steely determined expression on his face. He meant what he said. And said what he meant. "That's enough for now," he said. "If you want something to eat. There's food in the kitchen."

"Thank you," said Priskin. He waited for Asamovich to turn away from him and go through the door and out of view, then he went across the black and white tiles to another door on the other side. As he stepped across the floor he looked at the portraits on the wall. He could swear that the eyes followed him.

Asamovich's instruction was clear. Priskin had to discover who the purchaser was then make him an offer he couldn't refuse. He knew of people who would help him to achieve his boss's desires. He did lots of things for Yuri Asamovich. He supplied him with ladies of easy virtue. They were either Ukrainian, Bulgarian, or Romanian girls for whom Asamovich had a liking. His penchant was for a threesome with two girls. He liked to have sex with call-girls at least once a month when he would party, and champagne would flow into the early hours of the morning. The girls were very well paid so Asamovich was a popular client.

Asamovich was just one of several rich Russians who had made London their home. He had made a fortune in the aftermath of the collapse of the Soviet Union and communism. He had bought failing state-run companies for next to nothing, then he floated them on the newly created Moscow stock market. When the price of the shares went up he sold his holdings. In doing so he had made a lot of money. He had followed some of his contemporaries out of Russia to make a new life in London with his friends who had turned parts of South Kensington and other areas of London into, 'Moscow-by-the-Thames'. He had used a proportion of his wealth to buy works of art,

Faberge eggs, and classic cars which were housed in a garage in East London. He would occasionally go there to look at and sit in the cars. His favourite possessions were the three paintings he kept locked in a vault in the basement of the house: a Paul Gauguin original, a Van Gogh still-life, and a Monet landscape.

Chapter 3

Priskin opened the door and stepped into a spacious kitchen. Asamovich's trusted housekeeper and cook, Mrs Andropov was inside preparing some food for Asamovich's late supper. She was at least sixty-years-of-age. She greeted Priskin with a warm smile, then she gestured towards a table. "Have a seat," she said in Russian. "I have some Beluga Caviar. Or some Italian prosciutto and mozzarella cheese."

Priskin liked Mrs Andropov. She was easy to get along with. He sat at the kitchen table and scanned his eyes around the room, at the gleaming pans hanging from hooks on the end of metal cables inserted into the ceiling. Above the double sink and long draining board the fading light of the day was pressing at the window. A red tint had replaced the pink and orange colours in the sky.

Mrs Andropov poured him a cup of strong black Russian coffee, placed it onto a saucer and handed it to him. She had been Asamovich's trusted housemaid for the past twenty years. Ten of them in Moscow. Ten in London. Four less than the fourteen years Priskin had lived in London. As well as Priskin and Mrs Andropov, Asamovich employed a live-in valet. A Spanish man called Hector Valdes, who doubled as his chauffeur.

Priskin looked at his watch. The time was six o'clock. The clouds that had been threatening rain for the past hour, broke open and dropped a sprinkle of raindrops onto the window. He looked at his watch again. It was still six o'clock. He would leave it for an hour before calling a valuer he knew who worked for the auction house. She was an insider. She would tell him who had purchased the Faberge eggs. He would have to pay her for the information, but it would be a quick and easy method of discovering who had bought them. This is what Priskin did. He did jobs for Yuri Asamovich. For as well as being his financial advisor. He covered up for him: made enquiries on his behalf, asked questions, found women for him. He smoothed paths and massaged his towering ego. They were both Russians. Asamovich was from full white Russian stock. He was Moscow born and bred.

Priskin's father, Anatoli, worked for the Russian government in the period before Mikhail Gorbachev appeared on the scene. He had met a British woman who worked at the American school in Moscow. They met at a social event, fell in love, and married a year after in 1981. One year later, Dimitri was born in Moscow. Dimitri lived in Moscow with his parents. After ten years of a fractious relationship his parents divorced. His mother came back to England. Dimitri stayed in Moscow with his father, then came to England in 2001 at the age of nineteen to study at the University of London. His dual nationality allowed him to enter, then settle in the United Kingdom.

Mrs. Andropov made him a sandwich of the best Italian prosciutto and mozzarella cheese in crusty bread. As he munched the sandwich he contemplated his life. He wasn't rich, far from it. He had to work for a slime ball like Yuri Asamovich. How different to his life after leaving university in 2004. He got a job in the City of London working in the 'futures' market for a Russian bank. He had the job for three years. It was during this time that he first met Yuri. Yuri was impressed with his aptitude for numbers. He offered him a job which came with a salary of £150,000 per annum. That was eight years ago.

Priskin wasn't rich by Asamovich's standards, but he was comfortable. He had married Olga eight years ago. She was from St. Petersburg. He had met her at university and they formed a bond. They had a son, Andre, who was seven-years-of-age. Andre attended a private school in St. John's Wood. The fees were £8,000 a term. All paid for out of the money Asamovich paid Priskin to be his financial advisor and confidant.

Asamovich could grease palms and be a conduit between Moscow and London for politicians wishing to gain favour in either city. Priskin couldn't complain really. Asamovich paid well and the job was hardly full-time. He only worked when Asamovich wanted him to, which over fifty-two weeks of the year, three hundred and sixty-five days a year was roughly about twenty-five percent of the time. So, he had plenty of spare time for his family and pastimes, such as playing tennis and squash at a local sports club.

Dimitri Priskin was a studious learner. He knew far more about Asamovich then he let on. Like the fact that, at the beginning of Boris Yeltsin's reign in the Kremlin, Asamovich had embezzled a large amount of money out of a secret fund provided by the European Union to the Russian government. The problem for Asamovich was that a journalist from a Moscow newspaper began to investigate the whereabouts of the fund after he was tipped off by an EU delegate during a meeting in Brussels. The journalist began to dig for the truth to discover what had happened to the money. The journalist threatened to expose Asamovich and several other people. To make sure that this didn't happen, in 1998 Asamovich and the others had him shot dead in the doorway of the tenement building he lived in. Four years later, in 2002, Asamovich got out of Russia, bringing his Swiss bank account fortune with him. He settled in London. The British government didn't ask any questions. The influence of Russian money was having a beneficial effect on the British economy. Asamovich settled in Knightsbridge, then set about collecting works of art and cars and getting to know the great and the good of the British establishment. He still retained ties with people in high places back home in Russia. His alleged involvement in the murder of the journalist didn't go far. He was far too handy for people on both sides of the fallen iron curtain.

Priskin ate the sandwich Mrs Andropov had given him. It was getting on for one and half hours since he had left the auction. The paperwork pertaining to the sale of the two Faberge eggs would probably have been completed by now. He took his smart phone and found the number of Alexandra Baumer. She was the valuer at the auction house. He called the number. His call was answered on the fifth ring.

"Alexandra Baumer," she announced in a whispery soft tone of voice. Priskin got up onto his feet. He was one of those people who felt more comfortable, more in control standing, when talking on the telephone. It opened his nasal passage and allowed him to take in more oxygen into his lungs and to his brain. He took the brochure out of his pocket, opened it at page twenty-four and put his eyes on the glossy photograph of the two aquamarine objects.

"It's Dimitri Priskin," he said.

She hesitated. It had been a year or two since he had last spoken to her. Priskin thought she had the hots for him. She wasn't his kind. She was far too up her own backside and full herself. Right now, she did seem reluctant to talk to him.

"Err... What can I do for you?" she asked in a hushed voice. Maybe she was still in the office, above the auction floor.

"Can you talk?" he asked.

"Yes. But be quick."

"Lot eighteen. The two Faberge eggs."

"What about them?"

"Who purchased them?" he asked.

"Why do you need to know?" she asked, toying with him.

"A friend, Mr Watt, wants to know," he said. "He'll gladly pay for the information."

"Mr Watt?" she enquired, playing dumb.

"Fifty-pound notes, Mr Watt," said Priskin. "My boss wants to know who bought them. He'll give you plenty of Mr Watts."

"Mr Asamovich?"

"Huh uh," he said.

She didn't reply. There was a silence that lasted for a few long moments. He could hear voices around her. Maybe she was in the office. "I'll have to consult the records," she said softly.

"Please do that. When can I expect a call back?"

"In one hour from now," she replied with the hint of a question mark in her words.

"I look forward to speaking to you in one hour," Priskin said, then he terminated the call.

He slipped his smart phone into a pocket, then he took the crumb filled plate to the sink, ran it under the tap and placed it in a dish-holder on the draining board. Outside the dying embers of the red light in the sky were splashed for as far as the eye could see. The shrubs at the bottom of the garden were not visible. You could put three cricket pitches end-to-end on the garden and still have room to spare. Priskin disliked this time of the year. The early days of

October were always glum. It was uphill to Christmas. Spring was six months away. The thought made him feel depressed. Still it was warmer than it was in Moscow at this time of the year.

He left the Asamovich mansion, walked along the path to the end of the private road, stepped out through the security gate and onto Knightsbridge. He hailed a passing black cab to take him home to Notting Hill.

Chapter 4

Due to a road-traffic-accident on Bayswater Road, it took Priskin the best part of one hour to travel the one and a half miles from Knightsbridge to his home on the fringe of Notting Hill. By the time he arrived home his son Andre was already in his pyjamas. Olga had eaten. She asked him if he wanted anything to eat. He said he had had a sandwich and that he didn't have much of an appetite right now. He was more concerned about receiving the call from Alexandra Baumer, but he didn't tell his wife that. Asamovich's words about making the purchaser an offer he couldn't refuse were weighing heavy on his mind. Maybe he said it in jest. He did have a frivolous sense of humour at times. But maybe he meant it.

Olga told him they would have something to eat later, after she had put Andre to bed. She and Andre were about to tackle the homework he had brought home from school. He had to learn a passage from a book then recite it in class on Monday.

Olga was the love of his life. He had met her during a university night-out. They had dated a couple of times, then drifted apart before meeting up again at a housewarming party given by a mutual friend. The second time around she hadn't been looking for a lover, more of a male friend. Dimitri Priskin provided both. At five ten tall, slim, and dark haired he wasn't a bad catch. He had a Russian's pragmatic view of life.

Dimitri and Olga tended to speak Russian when they were alone together but spoke English with Andre. He had learned to speak Russian from an early age, but his parents only considered it right to speak English to him to help him with his schoolwork and build good English language skills.

Olga and Dimitri had settled down on the lounge sofa with Andre to tackle his homework before he went to bed. He had just completed the exercise when Priskin's smart phone sounded. He had almost forgotten that Alexandra Baumer had promised to call him back. He got up off the sofa, took his phone and stepped into the corridor. He didn't want Olga to hear the conversation. He accepted the call. It was Alexandra on the other end of the line.

"Have you got a name?" Priskin asked in a whisper.

"Yes," she replied. "There's a cost." She was already playing hard-ball with him.

"How much?" he asked.

"A thousand in cash," she replied.

"A thousand!" he exclaimed.

"A thousand," she repeated in a terse, tetchy manner.

Priskin cleared his throat. "Okay, if that's the price. I trust Yuri will be satisfied."

"I think so," she said.

"Why?" Priskin asked.

She didn't reply. "Can you meet me tomorrow afternoon?" she asked.

"Where?"

"Borough Market, close to London Bridge at three."

"Where in the market?" he asked.

"There's an oyster bar called, 'Oyster Catcher'. It's a sit-down. I'll be in there at the counter."

"Okay," said Priskin. She terminated the call. Priskin went back into the lounge to listen to his son read the entire page without one error.

Borough Market was busy at three o'clock on a Saturday afternoon. Tourists who had set out to walk across London Bridge from the north bank of the Thames to the south bank, often wandered into the market without knowing it was there. They were surprised to find a fully functioning indoor market that was perhaps one of the best in the whole of London, with its quaint stalls and vibe. The smell of spicy food, exotic cheeses and recently baked bread filled the air. As a breeze was blowing through the open entrance and exits it wasn't warm by any stretch of the imagination.

Priskin found the, 'Oyster Catcher'. He stepped inside and saw Alexandra Baumer sitting on a high stool by the counter. She had a dish of oysters in front of her. A glass of sparkling wine to a side. She was a rather goth like forty something with long dark hair and dark clothing. She was buxom and had too many blunt features to make her attractive. She clapped her eyes on Priskin has he entered. He slipped onto the stool next to her, glanced around the interior and put his eyes on a rather cute young blonde woman who was sitting at a table with an equally cute guy.

The girl assistant on the other side of the counter looked towards Priskin, but seeing Baumer acknowledge him, she moved away to the other side of the horseshoe shaped counter.

Priskin didn't care for oysters, or mussels or whelks or any other foodstuff that had once crawled in the ocean. She looked relaxed. Her green parka coat was lying on the top of the stool by her side. It didn't appear that she was working today, therefore she had plenty of time to meet with him. Her black handbag was sitting on the counter within easy reach.

"Have you brought the money?" she asked him straight out.

He dipped a hand into his coat pocket and extracted a wad of banknotes that were tightly wrapped inside a black plastic cover.

"Mr Watt says hello," he said. He placed the packet next to her. "A thousand," he said in a quiet voice. "Who bought the eggs?" he asked.

Before replying she looked to the table where the young couple were sitting. The couple were attractive, both blonde, tall and athletic looking. They were speaking a language that wasn't English. It may have been Dutch. Baumer took her eyes off the guy and put them back on Priskin. She considered his question for a few moments, then reached out and took hold of the packet. She could feel the wads of cash inside, but still opened it and peered inside.

"The guy's name?" Priskin asked.

Baumer give him the hint of a wicked smile. "Dale Farthing."

It was a name he didn't know. "Who?" he asked.

"Dale. Farthing. F.A.R.T.H.I.N.G," she spelt out the surname for him.

"Farthing?" Priskin asked.

"As in penny," she said.

"Penny?" he asked.

"Yes. His name is Farthing," she said, wishing she hadn't mentioned penny.

"Does he have an address?"

"He gave a certified address."

He didn't know what she meant by that. "What does that mean?" he enquired.

"It's his genuine address. He provided cast-iron evidence of his residence at this address."

"Which is?"

"Forty-eight. Dorset Gardens, Chelsea, SW1."

"Forty-eight. Dorset Gardens, Chelsea?" he repeated.

"Yes." She took hold of the packet containing the money and placed it inside her handbag.

"Has this Farthing purchased any items from you before?" he asked.

"First-timer… An auction virgin."

"What's his background?"

'No idea,' she said stiffly. She poked at an oyster on the plate with a fork. Priskin's nose puckered at the smell, then the sight of the slimy fish in the shell. It looked revolting.

"Are there any other people with the name Farthing, who buy items from your house?" he asked. He was determined to get his thousand pounds worth of information.

"Not as far as I am aware," she replied.

"Dave Farthing?" he said under his breath.

"No Dale." She pronounced the letter L with a roll of her tongue.

"Dale?"

"Yes."

"How did he pay for them?" he asked.

"By direct bank transfer," she replied.

"The full amount?"

"Yes."

"Who's got five hundred and sixty thousand to splash out on two eggs?"

"You'd be surprised. They're exquisite items. People want to buy exquisite things. Thing is though…" she said then paused.

"What?" asked Priskin, sensing she had a snippet of gossip to share.

"It's quite unusual for a first-time British buyer to pay that much."

Priskin gave her a puzzled expression. "What do you mean by that?"

"He's a first-time buyer spending five hundred and sixty thousand pounds."

"What are you getting at?" he asked. Uncertain of where she was going with this.

"Maybe he was buying for someone else."

Priskin sighed. "I see what you mean…Who?"

"Who knows," she replied. "It's becoming a common thing. People hide their purchase for a hundred different reasons."

"Such has?"

"Tax. Inheritance. Money laundering."

"Money laundering?" he asked with an exclamation in the tone.

"Yes, of course. People use dirty money to buy works of art."

"Interesting," said Priskin.

She took hold of an oyster shell, lifted it to her mouth and sucked down the content. The sound and sight almost made Priskin retch.

"It's not uncommon," she continued.

"How would you know if this guy was buying them with laundered money?"

"He's clean," she said.

"Clean?" How do you mean?"

"He doesn't have a police record. He's not a person of dishonest background. The money was transferred straight from his bank account into an auction house account so there's nothing suspect."

"How long will it be before he gets the eggs?" he asked.

"Monday. Probably," she replied.

"Okay," said Priskin. He tried to think of another question, but nothing came to mind. He didn't want to stick around for much longer. The smell of the oysters was getting to him and making him feel queasy. He slid off the stool. He didn't say another word except 'goodbye', then he walked out of the oyster bar and back into the middle of the market.

Dale Farthing. Forty-eight Dorset Gardens, he said to himself. From what he had seen of the man. Dale Farthing was a debonair, handsome, hirsute man with a confident manner. He may have never bought from an auction house before, but he had been to an auction before. He was savvy. He knew the score and never got caught out by the quick-fire bidding. There was no evidence to suggest that he was an auction virgin. Maybe he had been coached. Perhaps, he was buying the eggs for someone else. It was a possibility, but that's all it was, a possibility.

Priskin walked out of the market, turned to his left and headed out into the chill of the afternoon. He walked across London Bridge towards the north bank of the river. Behind him, the glass and steel shaft of the Shard soared skywards. The beautiful structure of Tower Bridge was to the right. Directly ahead the gleaming high-rise towers in the City of London were dotted across the skyline.

Once he was on the north bank of the river he hailed a black cab. He asked the driver to take him to Knightsbridge. He had an appointment to see Yuri Asamovich.

"Who bought the eggs?" Asamovich asked as soon as Priskin stepped into the room. He was in a light and airy conservatory at the back of the house, sitting in a hammock type of seat, gently rocking back and forth. Out through the French windows the garden was starting to lose its features in the dark shadow of the approaching evening. The bottle of Napoleon brandy on a side table by Asamovich had recently been opened. There was a small amount of the brownish liquid in the tumbler in his hand. He was wearing a chequered Pringle V-neck jumper and light slacks. Almost like the uniform of a golf pro. The collar of a green Polo neck shirt was visible at the rim. He put the edge of the glass to his lips and took a sip.

"A man called Dale Farthing," Priskin said, replying to his question.

Asamovich sucked on his teeth, then shrugged his shoulders gently. He put the glass on the side table. A blackbird landed on the grass outside, dug at the earth then took flight into one of the surrounding trees.

"Where does this fellow live?" Asamovich asked.

"At an address in Chelsea," Priskin replied. "Dorset Gardens. Off Oakley Street."

Asamovich had been in London long enough to know where Chelsea was, but not whether it was a posh part or somewhere not quite as nice as those little Mews thoroughfares and the smart wine-bars and bistros close to Cheyne Walk.

"You go to the house. Go in and find the eggs," Asamovich instructed. He was being deadly serious, for at times like this he very rarely said anything that could be construed to be a witticism. Laughter and fun were not things he indulged in unless he was in a jovial mood. Which he wasn't.

Priskin took in his instruction. Saying '*no I won't do it*' was not on the agenda. He considered his response carefully.

"I'll have to hire someone to break into the house," he said.

"Do it," replied Asamovich. "Find the eggs and bring them back to me." His tone was serious, and his face matched his words.

"According to the insider at the auction house. The eggs won't be released for a few more days."

"That's good," said Asamovich. "It gives you more time to plan."

"He may have purchased them for someone else," Priskin said.

"Like who?" Asamovich asked.

"I don't know," Priskin replied.

"Find out," said Asamovich. He shifted his weight to gently swing back and forth like a child on his favourite play-thing. The frame stretched and squeaked under the weight.

"I'll do that," said Priskin.

Under the circumstances there was little he could do. There was too much to risk. Too much at stake. Asamovich was too full of his own prestige to worry about Priskin's concerns. Priskin had to keep him sweet, to massage his ego and from time to time stroke his vision of his own self-importance. Asamovich took the brandy glass off the table and put the rim to his lips. He took a sip. "That's all," he announced.

Priskin stepped out of the conservatory and through the house to the front door. Asamovich's Bentley limousine was sitting on the peddled forecourt. The moonlight was reflecting in the gleaming bodywork and the sparkling glass.

Chapter 5

Priskin knew who to turn to for advice about breaking into forty-eight Dorset Gardens, Chelsea. He had, on several occasions, used the services of a man called Larry Mitchie for jobs like this. Mitchie was a Scot who had lived in London for the past twenty years. He worked as a freelance burglar for hire. If you had a reason and the finance, it was possible to call him to assist with a break-in. It was a rather odd way of making a living, but it wasn't his only line.

Mitchie's main occupation was as a maintenance engineer for a door company based in Wembley. He told Priskin he had worked for the British security service assisting them to break into the homes of those suspected of plotting terrorist activity against the state. Whilst he had never actually provided any evidence Priskin had no reason to disbelieve him. He had used him on a couple of occasions some time ago. The last time was when he had tracked down a photographer who had taken several photographs of Yuri Asamovich leaving a Mayfair casino at three in the morning with a lady on his arm. Another associate of Priskin, a private detective called Ron Alwyn, had contacted Mitchie and hired him to break into the small business unit of the wannabe paparazzi, so he could give him a good hiding. The photographer had both of his arms broken in the ensuing attack. The guy never took another photograph in his life.

This was going to be a lot different, then it had been on a business unit in Ealing, this was a house in an up-market residential part of Chelsea.

Priskin planned to call Mitchie this evening and ask him to meet with him in a mutually agreed venue to talk about a job. Asamovich had made his mind up. He was determined to have the eggs and pay not one penny for them.

Priskin called Mitchie, using the mobile telephone number he had for him. They agreed to meet in a spot outside of Earls Court underground station on Warwick Road, or as it was more informally known, the exhibition hall side of the station.

It was eight o'clock on a chilly, rain filled Sunday evening. The breeze blowing along Warwick Road was edged with a fine spray of drizzle that had been falling since the early afternoon. Traffic zoomed along the one-way section of the road. In the distance were a set of traffic lights at the junction of the A4 and Cromwell Road. The streetlights were reflecting in the sheen of wet on the road and in the rain drenched gutter.

Priskin was wearing a knee length dark raincoat. He had a dark flat cap on his head pulled low. He walked along Warwick Road in a northerly direction from the Brompton side of Earls Court. He dug his hands into the pockets of the raincoat and dropped his head to shield his face against the sheet of damp. Up ahead, in the near distance the familiar, red, white, and blue, circular shape of the illuminated sign of the underground station shone bright against the gloom. The entrance to the station was not too far.

Mitchie said he would be standing outside the newspaper vendor stall which would be boarded-up at this time of the evening. There were few people around, except for the thin line of commuters coming out of the station exit. The rain and the cold breeze had certainly deterred many people from heading out this evening.

As he neared the sign, Priskin could make out the figure standing by the covered walkway that led into the station. As he got nearer to the entrance he could see Mitchie standing by the stall. He was a short, squat guy, perhaps only five feet five tall. He was wearing a thick dark jacket that came level to his thighs. A black leather flat cap on his head. The extended peak was pulled low, much like Priskin's own head gear. The brown leather gloves on his hands were arranged into tight fists. The tip of a cigarette in his mouth glowed against the pallid colour of flesh on his chubby face. He looked up as Priskin came into view, then he flicked the wet end of the cigarette into the air and sent it cartwheeling into the rain-soaked gutter.

At five ten tall, Priskin towered over him, whereas Mitchie was far wider and far more solid than him. It wasn't excess fat. It was all muscle and solid chest.

"Eh, what's the score?" he asked in a Glaswegian accent that was still strong despite living in the south of England for the past twenty years. "Geez. I'm fair nithered," he said. He hopped from one leg to the other as if he was performing some type of highland fling or standing on red hot coals.

"It's a break-in at a house not far from here," said Priskin.

"Whereabouts?"

"Dorset Gardens in Chelsea."

Mitchie looked interested. "What's the need?" he asked.

"I'm looking for something," Priskin said.

"Such has?"

Priskin was going to say mind your own business but thought better of it. "Two Faberge eggs," he replied. "I also need to find out more about this guy."

"Who?"

"Someone called Dale Farthing," said Priskin.

"Okay," said Mitchie.

He had stopped hopping from side to side. A commuter emerged out of the covered exit and stepped out into the wet, blaspheming as he saw it was still chucking it down. Overhead, the sky had a grey tint in it, so it doused everything in that colour. In the background the sound of a tube train either entering or leaving the station was audible. A bus came hurtling along Warwick Road, seeking to get through the lights at the junction before they changed from green to red.

"How do you want to tackle it?" Priskin asked.

"Check it out first. I'll do a recce," said Mitchie.

"A what?"

"A reconnaissance. Get a look at it. Check it out.   See what's what. What's the address?" Mitchie asked.

"Forty-eight, Dorset Gardens, Chelsea. Off Oakley Street," Priskin replied.

"I know it. It's a new development. Been there for a couple of years. Big executive type homes, with a mews on each end of the street. Private road access." He took his hands out of his pockets, then gently rocked back and forth on the balls of his feet.

"When do we do the job?" he asked.

"We?" said Priskin.

"I guess, you're coming along for the ride?" Mitchie asked, surprised.

Priskin waited for a moment before replying. "Yeah, I want to be there with you."

"All righty. As you wish. Come along for the buzz," said Mitchie.

"Something like that," said Priskin. "As soon as."

"Middle of next week Wednesday or Thursday," Mitchie said.

"Sooner rather than later," Priskin said.

"Forty-eight Dorset gardens?" Mitchie asked. Priskin nodded his head. "I'll do the recce. Let you know the SP."

"The what?"

"The starting price."

"Your fee?" Priskin asked.

"Same as before. A grand." In his Scottish accent the word 'grand' sounded wonderful.

"Okay. A grand. Call me," said Priskin. He dipped a hand into a pocket and extracted a business card size piece of paper. It had an eleven-digit telephone number written on it in thick black ink. "That's my new number."

Mitchie took the card in his gloved hand and slotted it into his pocket before the rainwater had chance to smudge the ink. Priskin watched him turn and walk into the glass covered passage and head towards the ticket barrier before the stairs going down to the platforms. Priskin turned and walked back the way he had come. He had parked his car, a Kia 4x4, on a street close to Brompton cemetery.

Chapter 6

Forty-eight hours passed. It was Tuesday night. Priskin was at home in Notting Hill. He had just put Andre to bed at eight o'clock and had just settled down in his study to do some work for Asamovich. Olga was in the kitchen with a glass of red wine in her hand, flicking through the glossy pages of a fashion magazine.

Priskin loved her dearly. She was the mother of his son. She was his soul partner and he hers. He wished he could provide a lot more for her and be able to afford some of the high-end clothes she saw in the magazines. They had talked about having another child, but she said Andre was enough. In the intervening years since the birth of Andre she had gone off sex at a steadily increasing rate. He put it down to early menopause. No matter she still loved him, and he loved her.

Priskin had taken her back to St Petersburg on two occasions to visit her mother who still lived in the city. She had been in London for the same period of time as him. Maybe one day they would return to live in Russia. He wanted to be wealthy. He lived in a nice part of central London, but he wasn't as wealthy as some of those who lived nearby. He didn't have anywhere near the two hundred million pounds Yuri Asamovich had amassed through his dodgy deals. Two hundred million was still way off the wealth of some Russians who had come to live in London in the years before and after the millennium. If he had a hundredth of Asamovich's fortune Priskin would be a happy man.

On this Tuesday evening he was sitting in his study working at his computer. The spreadsheet on the screen was a review of his own personal fortune which was just a shade shy of three quarters of a million pounds. He closed the page as his smart phone sounded. It was Larry Mitchie calling. He took the call, after first making sure that the door to the room was closed tight.

"What have you got?" he asked Mitchie.

Mitchie told him that he had done a recce on the area and the house at forty-eight Dorset Gardens. It was in that new development. Just along Oakley Street. It was a fine, detached home, two floors high, modern design. All stone block, big windows, and a turreted roof. It could be accessed down a private road running off Oakley Street. The property had a narrow segment of space running down the sides and a mid-size garden to the front and rear.

Mitchie said the best way to gain entry onto the property was via the wall at the rear of the house. The wall could be accessed by a walkway that ran parallel to the rear of the houses on either side. The walkway linked two mews thoroughfares at each end of the block of detached homes. The wall was only six feet high. On the other side of the wall was a garden then the back of the house. There was an area of decking by a patio door. An alarm box was visible on both the front and back elevations. When he had gone to the house today, in the afternoon, all the blinds over the windows were down, which suggested to him that the occupants were not at home.

He had got onto the property through a front gate in a wrought iron fence and completed a quick look around. The door to the garage attached to the side of the house on the left side was closed. A black Maserati sports car was visible through dusty windows. The shrubs in the glazed plant pots by the front door and on the decking looked healthy. At the front of the house was a brick tile forecourt with the space to park a couple of decent size vehicles. At the back, next to the patio was a second single door that led into the house. Mitchie even referred to a cat-flap in the door. There was no evidence of a build-up of post in the letter-box that was attached to the iron fence at the front.

Mitchie talked for a while. Priskin was conscious of the need to cut him off at some point as he didn't want him to talk all night. "Let's cut this short," he advised. "What do you recommend?"

Mitchie recommended an early morning attempt to break into the house, through the patio door at the rear. Access onto the property could be made down the walkway, then over the brick wall and into the garden. Priskin asked him for a timescale.

"Thursday morning," said Mitchie.

Priskin ruminated on it for a few moments. "Sounds okay," he said. "Where?"

"Where what?" Mitchie asked.

"Where shall we meet and what time?"

"Same place as before. Outside of Earls Court. I'll have someone drive us to the house," said Mitchie.

"Who?" Priskin asked.

"A friend," replied Mitchie quickly. Priskin didn't want to ask him who. The less he knew the better. Mitchie continued. "He'll come for us. We'll have one hour to get into the house and find the things you're looking for," he said.

Priskin didn't respond. It sounded as if Mitchie had given it plenty of consideration. "Okay," said Priskin. "What time?"

"Let's make it one-forty-five outside of Earls Court. Same place."

"Thursday morning?" Priskin asked for confirmation.

"That's right. One-forty-five," replied Mitchie in his broad Glaswegian accent.

There was a knock at the door to the study. It was Olga. "I've got to go," said Priskin to Mitchie in a whisper. "Thursday morning. See you then," he said then he terminated the conversation and put his smart phone down. "Come in," he said in a raised voice.

The door opened. Olga put her head around the frame and looked at him. She opened the door wide, stepped inside, yawned, and raised her arms high above her head in such a way that her boobs rose ever so slightly. She still had a lovely figure.

"Who were you speaking to?" she asked.

"Guess?"

"Yuri."

"Go it in one," he replied. "He wants me to accompany him to an all-night poker game with some of his friends who live in Mayfair. It will be an all-nighter."

"When?"

"Wednesday night into Thursday morning,"

She said nothing. She perhaps suspected her husband was having an affair and that was her on the phone, but in truth she knew he had been faithful to her since the day he said his vows in the Russian Orthodox church in Chiswick where they were married. He shrugged his shoulders. Her face had a red glow to it. The whites of her eyes were glazed. She must have had several more glasses of wine than usual. She came to him and wrapped her arms around his shoulders and across his chest.

"вообразить раннюю ночь?" *fancy an early night?* she said and nibbled on his ear lobe.

Priskin logged off, then turned the PC off.

Chapter 7

Priskin hadn't seen or spoken to Yuri since their last meeting four days ago. He didn't feel it appropriate to inform him what he had learned or what the plan was going forward.

On Wednesday evening he left his home at a shade after midnight. He drove to the Earls Court area. It took him twenty minutes to drive the two-mile distance by doing it in a roundabout route. The night was breezy, but dry, just like the day had been. The high winds and rain of the past few days had eased, though it was still gusting and sending litter swirling in a spin. The first storm of the autumn had moved across the southern half of the United Kingdom. It would soon be out over the English Channel and reaping havoc to shipping on the high seas.

He parked his white, nearly new Kia 4x4 car, on a quiet street in Earls Court in a secluded area of red brick blocks of flats. He settled down to wait for the time to pass. He was wearing a black sweater, under a dark sports zip-up jacket and black jogging pants.

Thirty minutes passed. It looked as if most of the occupants of the flats in the immediate vicinity had settled down for the night so there wasn't any movement, though the traffic on Warwick Road at the end of the thoroughfare was still busy at this hour. A night bus, half full of passengers, came by.

A further thirty minutes passed. At a time, close to one-thirty he got out of the car, closed the door gently, then set off to walk the three hundred yards to the underground station. At the junction with Warwick Road he glanced to the right to see the traffic lights at the junction with the A4. The glow in the supermarket across the junction threw a pool of illumination across the road. A night bus was stationary at a bus stop. Its hazards were flashing on and off, for a reason that wasn't immediately apparent. He turned left and walked along the path towards the underground station entrance. The path was deserted. Not a soul was around. The breeze sent a discarded coffee container scurrying along the road.

On the other side of the thoroughfare the drab, high, semi-circular concrete facade of Earls Court exhibition hall loomed high above the road. Priskin felt a mixture of excitement and dread at the thought of breaking into Farthing's home. Breaking in and entering someone's house was not something he did on a regular basis. It was an offence. It was serious business. If the police caught him in the act he could expect to find himself in heaps of trouble.

He waited outside of the walkway leading into the station. The entrance into the station was open though the trains had ceased running for the night.

It was one-forty-five when a car came along the road. Instead of zooming towards the traffic-lights the vehicle pulled into the kerb and reduced speed. Priskin didn't notice the make or the model of the vehicle. They all looked the same to him. He couldn't tell one vehicle from the other. The vehicle came to a halt. Under the glare of the streetlights he couldn't make out the colour of the bodywork. Through the windscreen he could see two figures in the front seats. Larry Mitchie was in the passenger seat, sitting next to the driver whom Priskin didn't know.

He stepped forward, opened the back door on the driver's side and slipped onto the back seat. The interior had a new feel and smell, that nice fragrance of fresh upholstery and imitation leather. Gangster rap was playing out of the speakers.

The driver put his foot on the gas and sped up the road to the start of the A4 to the left and Cromwell Road to the right. The continuation of Warwick Road was straight on through the junction. Though Priskin couldn't see the driver from behind he looked like a young guy. He was wearing a baseball cap on his head. Ringlets of long corkscrew hair were escaping out from underneath the elasticated rim. Mitchie didn't bother to introduce the driver. There was a smell of stale cigarette smoke. It lingered with the smell of the new plastic trim to give a strange sickly combination.

Mitchie turned to face Priskin. "Here take these," he advised. He passed him three items, one at a time. They were a pair of black leather gloves and a woven garment. It took him a few moments to see it was a full-face balaclava. "Can't be too careful," Mitchie said. "Put them on as soon as we get there."

Suddenly the reality of what they were about to attempt dawned on Priskin. They really were going to break into a house. As the driver approached the traffic lights at the top of Warwick Road he got into the righthand lane. The light was on red. The morning was dark and windswept. The lights in the supermarket on the corner were ablaze. There was one person standing in the open doorway. When the traffic lights changed from red to green the driver turned right onto Cromwell Road and headed towards central London. A local authority wagon was trundling along the road with its hazard lights flashing. Workmen in luminous orange jackets had erected a tent in the middle of the left-hand lane. Despite the early hour maintenance staff were working, taking advantage of the lack of traffic to do essential repairs to the road surface. Priskin slipped the gloves over his hands. He didn't bother with the balaclava just yet.

At the next junction the driver turned right onto Earls Court Road and on towards Brompton. It was getting on for ten-to-two. The shop fronts along the road were lit up, though some were hidden behind metal shutters. An all-night café was empty, but for a staff member, standing behind the counter waiting to serve a customer. The door to an all-night pharmacy slid open and a couple of guys came out carrying a paper bag. Several cars came the other way, but in general there were few people out on the streets of west London at two o'clock in the morning.

At the junction with Kings Road, the driver turned right and headed along the road. The plush residences of Chelsea and South

Kensington were soon in reach. At the junction with Oakley Street the driver headed towards the pillars of Albert Bridge in the distance. After a hundred yards he pulled up adjacent to the narrow entrance to a 'private access only' road. They had reached the inlet leading to Dorset Gardens. A notice on a lamp-post was headed, *'The Royal Borough of Kensington and Chelsea'* and said: *'Private Road, no through road. Dorset Gardens, leading to Calista Mews.'*

"You ready?" Mitchie asked Priskin. He didn't wait for Priskin to reply. He opened the passenger door and swung his feet out. Priskin followed him. He still had the balaclava in his hand. Mitchie had a cigar shaped canvas bag in his hand that contained the tools of the trade. The driver didn't wait for instructions. As soon as the two of them were out of the vehicle he set off, up the road, towards Albert bridge.

Mitchie led Priskin into the narrow inlet to the private road. Nothing stirred. The light in several mock Edwardian lampposts lit the scene in a dim haze. The light was so poor it hardly registered on the surface of the cobble stones. At the end of the inlet Mitchie turned left and stepped onto a narrow mews street, there were small cottages on one side. The back-to-back houses on Dorset Gardens were ahead, set out in a rectangular shape. A path dissected down the middle to cut the two sides in half.

They were soon at an iron gate leading onto the path. The gate was not only closed but padlocked. Mitchie delved into the canvas bag. He extracted a pair of bolt cutters and placed the jaws against the padlock bolt. He held it there until the jaws were tight then he applied the necessary force to cut through the iron. The bolt snapped clean in two. Priskin took the padlock and wrenched it free.

"Put that on," advised Mitchie referring to the balaclava. Priskin did has told. He put the opening over his head and pulled it down to cover his face. The two eye sockets allowed him to see. Something in an overhanging tree made a sound. The breeze got up and made a rustling sound in the branches. A pile of fallen leaves was scattered across the ground, carpeting the floor in a cushion underlay. Priskin couldn't recall being so high on adrenalin in a long time. He felt a buzz that quickened his reactions and movements. He stepped through the now open gate. Mitchie followed Priskin and closed the gate behind him. He made sure the metal bolt was all the way in the catch.

Moving forward along the path they moved in a scurrying motion. The tools in Mitchie's bag made a jingle-jangle sound. After forty yards they were at the brick wall that formed the boundary between the walkway and the rear of the Farthing property.

Larry Mitchie may have been small, but he was very strong and agile. He put the tool bag onto the flat top of the wall, then hitched his legs up the bricks and pulled himself onto the top of the wall in no time. Priskin had to take a run-up, thrust his hands up, grab the top of the ridge and pull himself up.

By the time he was clambering onto the flat ridge, Mitchie was already on the other side of the wall. Priskin managed to get a firm hold, pull his legs up, twist around and drop down to the other side. He fell, feet first, into a heap of compost. Mitchie had to stifle a guffaw in his throat. Priskin swore in Russian, then cursed Asamovich. Mitchie said nothing. He took hold of the bag, then running in long, stealthily strides he went across the lawn to the back of the house. The radiant moonlight was splashed across the grass like a spotlight highlighting an outdoor stage.

Priskin joined Mitchie on the wood decking by the patio door. Mitchie opened the tool bag. He extracted a pencil torch and a battery-operated drill. A bit was already attached into the nozzle. Vertical blinds were closed over the glass doors. There was no obvious indication that anyone was at home.

"Hold this on the door," said Mitchie. He passed the pencil torch to Priskin. "Put it on the lock," he added.

Priskin did has requested. As he breathed out the air in his lungs instantly turned to steam.

"What about the alarm?" he asked.

"What about it?"

"How are you going to turn it off?"

"It's an internal alarm. Not external. If no one is at home, no one will hear it," he said.

"Okay," said Priskin. "But what if someone is?"

"Then we'll have a problem."

Mitchie turned the drill on and aimed the tip of the bit at the keyhole. It wasn't long before the bit was cutting into the metal. It made little sound. After a few minutes, he turned the drill off, and placed it on the decking. Then he took hold of the handle and gave it a firm yank. The door opened to a gap of approximately two centimetres before the bolts locked tight. Next, Mitchie took a chisel from his bag, placed the top edge against the first of the three bolts and lodged it underneath. Using sheer brute strength, he forced the first of the bolts out of the frame. There were two more bolts. He had to repeat the procedure twice, before he managed to get the bolts out of the frame. It was free after five minutes of energy sapping force.

Mitchie seemed to hesitate for a moment. Perhaps he wasn't one hundred percent sure that the alarm system wasn't external. If it sounded they would have to flee. Though Priskin hadn't seen a 'neighbour watch' notice, a neighbour was bound to investigate a ringing alarm.

Before opening the door, Mitchie delved into his bag. He withdrew a pair of short handle wire cutters. "I'll go in," he said. "Tackle the alarm if it goes off. You stay out here."

"What?" asked Priskin.

Mitchie ignored him. Priskin didn't have much of an option, but to go along with it. He watched Mitchie take the door, slide it open, push the blind to a side and enter the house. There was an instant blur-blur-blur of an alarm going off inside the house. Priskin closed the patio-door to drown out the sound. He stepped back to look up onto the upper floors. If there was anyone in the house the noise would have woken them by now. He anticipated an upstairs light coming on, but it never happened.

Minutes passed before Mitchie returned. He opened the door. The sound of the alarm had ceased. "I've managed to disconnect the alarm box," he announced gleefully.

"How?" Priskin asked.

"Tricks of the trade," he replied.

"Is it safe?" Priskin asked.

"Of course," Mitchie said. "Come on let's find what we've come for."

"Two Faberge eggs," said Priskin.

Mitchie returned inside the house. Priskin followed him. He stepped through the door and entered. The interior was dark. They were in a room that was dominated by a large dining table and chairs. The only light source was from the thin beam shining out of the end of the torch in Mitchie's hand. He had been correct about the alarm system. It was internal only.

They said nothing. There was no plan as such, only to look for the two eggs. At the end of the dining room were a pair of pine louvre doors that opened into another room. This was a lounge come living room that faced the front of the house. It had a large L shape sofa against a side wall with several armchairs dotted here and there. There didn't seem much in the way of embellishment or ornaments, but it was tricky to see in the dark. From what Priskin could tell the furniture looked expensive and modern. There was a large gold and glass doomed ornamental carriage clock sitting on the top of a sideboard and picture frames on the walls. Mitchie put the beam around the room and let it settle on a picture frame above a wide, open fireplace. As the beam picked out the features of the painting it looked to Priskin like a distinctive landmark he knew. Unless he was very mistaken, it was the front of the Winter Palace in St. Petersburg. He may have been wrong, but it looked very similar. It had to be an original oil on canvas painting.

Mitchie took the beam off the painting, then put it on the wide TV screen on the opposite wall. There was no obvious smell of cooked food or any sound. In the dark it was spooky and eerie. Mitchie let the beam go around the room, then he stepped across the wood floor towards another pair of louvre doors and opened them. They stepped into another room. This was set up as a study. There was a large desk backed against one side. An all-in-one PC on the work surface and a HP printer. A high-back leather office chair was in front of the desk. A pair of metal cabinets each with three drawers were by a window that looked out on the side of the house and the garage. There were no carpets, just thick rugs over bare varnished floorboards.

After a couple of minutes, they began the search for the Faberge eggs. They had no desire to trash the house. Far from it. They went through the rooms, opening what drawers there were. They searched diligently. If they took anything out of a drawer, they put it back in the same place they had found it.

From the lounge Priskin went into a hallway that led to the front door. He turned down the corridor, went through another door and into a kitchen. By habit he reached for a light switch and inadvertently turned a ceiling light on. Panels in the ceiling flickered into life. The illumination revealed a plethora of modern appliances like a double sink and silver drainer, a massive stand-alone Smeg fridge and freezer with an ice and drinks dispenser in the door. There was a central work table with a secondary sink unit. Shiny white surfaced cupboards were on the walls. Priskin heard a sound of something moving behind the table. He looked down to see a cat stroll by. The animal stopped and put a pair of turquoise eyes on him. It had a coat of thick grey fur. It had a thin band of a collar around its neck.

Priskin had no great knowledge of cats, but it did resemble a Russian Blue. The cat let out a meow, then moved off again before once again pausing to look at him.

Mitchie came into the room, cursing. He instantly reached for the switch and turned it off to plunge the room back into dark. "What you're doing?" he asked bluntly.

Priskin didn't reply to his question. "Did you see that cat?" he asked.

"What?"

"The cat," said Priskin.

"Never mind about a fucking cat. Stop been a prat," he chastised, which coming from Mitchie sounded funny.

Mitchie backed out of the room. He went down the corridor to the stairs near to the front door. Priskin followed him. They both ascended to the upper floor. Once in the main bedroom they began to search through the drawers in a chest and cupboards. Again, they replaced everything and were conscious not to upset anything. They went from room to room. In the main bedroom the double bed was king-size. There were tables on both sides each with a large reading lamp on it. Above the bed was a glass frame that contained a photograph of a happy couple on their wedding day.

By now nearly thirty minutes had passed. In several drawers in a chest Priskin found a lot of female underwear, all bearing the label, 'Victoria's Secret.'

There was a walk-in wardrobe in the main bedroom, which housed men's jackets on one side and female clothing on the other. Priskin put an internal light on. There were at least two dozen pairs of both men's and ladies' shoes. There were also several dozen handbags, along with several Harrods' shopping bags. The Farthings appeared to be wealthy and by the clothing on display, equally well attired.

Priskin searched through the drawers in an antique chest. He put his hand through garments to feel for the hidden Faberge eggs. He didn't find them. He opened another door and stepped into an on-suite bathroom. There were white fluffy towels on the edge of a deep bath and over the glass door of a shower cubicle. He opened a cabinet door and looked in there for the eggs.

From the bathroom he went into a second bedroom which housed a double bed that looked as if it hadn't been slept in for some time. The high-quality furniture was just as tasteful as the other rooms. What he did notice was the lack of a child's room or children's toys and clothing.

After a further fifteen minutes of searching they had found nothing of value. Priskin went down the stairs. Mitchie was sitting on the bottom step. He had stopped searching. Mitchie shone the torch into his face. "Find them?" he enquired.

Priskin raised his hand to shield his eyes from the glare of the light. He shook his head. "Nothing, but a lot of very expensive gear, like Versace suits and Yves-Saint Lauren clothing," he replied.

"We've only got another ten minutes," said Mitchie.

Priskin didn't respond. He stepped forward, then paused having lost his orientation for a moment. He took the door that led into the kitchen, opened it, and stepped inside. The moonlight was streaming in through the window, reflecting on the shiny aluminium surface of the sink and drainer. He felt something brush passed his feet and looked down to see the cat idle by him. It went onto the stairs and jumped onto the first step, alongside Mitchie who was now standing, leaning against the bannister.

"Give me the torch," asked Priskin. Mitchie handed it to him. He put the beam on and shone it around the kitchen and placed it onto the door of the tall fridge. The door was festooned with magnets. He went across to the unit and looked at them. One caught his eye. It said: 'I luv SP'. Another one had the white, blue, and red tricolour of the Russian flag on it. Not for the first time Priskin wondered if there was a Russian connection to the owners of the home.

Mitchie came into the kitchen. "What you going to do?" he asked. "Give up?"

"Not sure," said Priskin. "The eggs aren't here. It might take days to find them."

Mitchie sniffed. "That's true. So, what you going to do?" he asked for a second time.

"I'm going to take something else?"

"Like what?" Mitchie asked.

"The cat."

"What?"

"The cat."

"The cat? Why?" Mitchie asked. "You can't be serious?" he added.

"Don't ask."

Priskin went out of the door to the bottom of the stairs. The cat was loitering on the fifth step. He gently stepped up the stairs, got behind the cat, reached down, then cupped his hand under the animal's soft belly and lifted it off its feet. It tried to dig its claws into the carpet to prevent him from lifting it, but it soon gave up. It didn't protest or make a sound. It was a cat that liked to be picked up and pampered. It didn't protest or wriggle as he stroked its deep, dense fur. It purred and twisted its head to look at him through its big opal blue and green eyes.

He took a firm hold of it and carried on up the stairs, went into the main bedroom and into the walk-in wardrobe. He took one of the Harrods' shopping bags, opened it and placed the cat inside. Before it could attempt to climb out he closed the zip. Then he went down the stairs with the cat in the bag.

"What've got in the bag?" Mitchie asked, maybe thinking he had found the Faberge eggs.

"The cat," he replied. Mitchie tutted as if he thought Priskin was crazy but he said nothing. "Let's go," said Priskin.

"You're the boss," replied Mitchie in his deadpan vernacular.

Priskin walked through the lounge, into the dining room, through the patio door and outside onto the decking. Mitchie followed him out and closed the door behind him. They had left the house as they had found it. Nothing had been taken except for a fluffy cat.

They were soon out in the garden and climbing over the brick wall. Once in the walkway between the backs of the houses they ventured along the path to the gate. Overhead the sky was clear. The moonlight framed the scene as it cut through the bare spindly branches of the trees.

Within a minute they were at the end of the passageway and stepping out onto the cobblestone mews. The cat was jumpy in the bag. Its weight pulled down on Priskin's arms so much so that he had to use an arm to support the bag. It made a series of meows then it settled down before jumping again.

From the mews they moved onto the inlet to the private road, then right at the end and onto Oakley Street. Over to the left, illumination was splashed onto the pillars of Albert Bridge, which was around two hundred yards from where they were standing in the shadows. They had to wait five minutes for the driver to return to collect them.

Priskin was going back to the street in Earls Court to collect his car. All he had to show for his night's work was a shiny green Harrods' bag containing a cat. No Faberge eggs. He had no idea where they could be. The significant information he had discovered were the Monet like oil-on-canvas painting that resembled the Winter Palace in Saint Petersburg. The 'I Luv SP 'and the White, red, and blue Russian flag fridge magnets. Did the Farthings have a Russian connection? He was intrigued.

Chapter 8

"Dimitri Priskin," shouted Olga from downstairs. Priskin knew he was in trouble. When Olga called him by his full name he was usually in bother. He was still in bed. He glanced at the bedside clock. The time was eight o'clock. The light of the morning was filtered by the closed blinds over the window.

"What?" he asked in a raised voice.

"What's this?" she shouted from the bottom of the stairs.

"Oh yeah." He got out of bed, grabbed the robe on the bedside chair and slipped it on, tightening the sash cord around his waist as he stepped to the door. He opened the door, went onto the landing, and down the stairs at a slow descent. He could hear a commotion in the kitchen and Andre's excited squeals of delight. "Mummy. It's a cat," he said breathlessly as if he'd been chasing the animal around the kitchen for the last two minutes.

Priskin made it down to the bottom of the stairs and went into the kitchen. "I was going to tell you about that," he said, "but you were asleep."

Olga was standing by the door, looking pensive, as if she had just seen a rat, not a beautiful cat. "Whose cat is it?" she asked.

"No idea," he replied. "It was by the gate when I came in this morning. It was freezing this morning, so I brought it in and put it down by the radiator. I couldn't leave it out there."

"Mummy. It's a cat," repeated Andre. He was still in his pyjamas. A smile as wide as the River Thames on his face. The cat now minus its collar, remained seated, watching them - watching him. It didn't bat an eyelid as the chaos ensued around him. He knew he was King. He didn't have any need to worry. Someone would always love him and care for him no matter what. Someone would pamper him to the day he died.

"On the path outside the gate?" Olga asked as if she was having trouble believing him.

"Yeah, right outside on the path," he said in a definite tone and pitch of voice. It was doubtful if she believed him. Andre had gotten over his initial hesitation. He approached the cat, held his hand out and gave its fur a long stroke. The cat arched his back. Andre was besotted. He had a pet for the first time in his life.

"Daddy can we keep it?" he asked.

"It's not our cat," said his mother.

Sanity seemed to have prevailed for the moment. "We'll have to see," said Priskin, which drew a stern facial rebuke from Olga.

"He could be someone else's pet," she said, addressing them both.

Priskin's decision to take off the collar had been a wise one. "He doesn't have a collar," he said.

"Maybe it fell off. Anyway, what time did you get in this morning?" she asked changing the subject.

"At around three. I had to take Yuri home from the casino in Mayfair."

She didn't say a word.

"Mummy. Daddy. Can we keep the cat?" Andre asked again in an excited tone.

"We'll have to find out if anyone has lost a cat," his mummy said.

"If they have we'll have to take it back," said his dad. "They'll want him back. If you don't cry, I'll take you to the cat's home and we'll get you a cat of your own. Is that a deal?" Priskin asked his son.

Andre reflected on his dad's words. His mum said nothing. "All right daddy," said Andre like a brave little soldier.

"What does he eat?" Olga asked.

"Cat food. You buy it in a supermarket," said Priskin, then wished he hadn't said it like that. He yawned, then ran a hand through his hair. The time was only eight o'clock. He wanted to go back to bed. His wife looked daggers at him. Andre saved the day by stroking the cat. It purred, then shot off into the dining room with Andre and Olga in hot pursuit. Priskin smiled to himself, then the reality dawned on him. He had to return the cat to its rightful owners, but not just yet. He would keep it for a while. A few days at least.

It was three in the afternoon when Priskin received a call from Asamovich. His boss wanted to see him in one hour. Three of his friends were flying into London from Moscow on Friday to meet with him. Priskin had to get some things organised. It sounded as if the meeting had been planned for some time, but this was the first time he had been told about it. The secretive world of Asamovich was becoming a regular occurrence.

Priskin was at the house in Knightsbridge within the hour. Asamovich greeted him in the round reception room just inside the entrance. He took him through to the lounge. He was dressed casually in one of the many cashmere Pringle golf jumpers he owned, over a shirt that was aquamarine in colour. The smell of a recently smoked Montecristo cigar was in the air. He must have put it out in the three minutes Priskin had been waiting at the door.

Asamovich had his smart phone in his hand as if he had been consulting the FTSE 100 to see if the index was up or down on the day's trading. He had an excellent acumen for stocks and shares and often sold his shares in a falling bear market, then bought them back at a lower price in anticipation of a 'dead-cat-bounce'. He sat on a Chesterfield sofa as Priskin remained standing. "Did you trace the Faberge eggs?" he asked.

"I broke into the purchaser's home this morning, but there was no trace of them," he replied. Asamovich considered his words. His expression was neutral. There was neither a smile or a frown on his face which was usually a signal that he was disappointed with the answer he'd just been given.

"How much did it cost?" he asked.

"One thousand," Priskin replied.

"Take it from the usual source," said Asamovich. The usual source was a fund Priskin had access to for such things as hiring criminals and prostitutes for his boss. "I need you to do something," Asamovich said reverting to Russian. Priskin didn't reply.

"I have three friends coming from Moscow on Friday. Get me four girls for a party. That girl called Monica will do, and three others."

Priskin nodded his head. Monica was the name of a pretty blonde, Ukrainian girl he had found for Asamovich. She had been to the house on two previous occasions and had spent the night with Asamovich. "What time do you want the girls to arrive?" he asked.

"Ten o'clock," he replied. Priskin knew a party was going to be held here. Mrs Andropov was in the kitchen already preparing the food for a banquet. There was the best wild red salmon from Harrods, which was only six hundred metres away from the house. A case of Dom Perignon champagne at one hundred and fifteen pounds a bottle and several hampers from Fortnum and Mason.

72

"I'll speak to Monica," he said. "I'll ask her to bring three other girls with her on Friday night. All blondes and young."

"Good," said Asamovich. "Make the necessary arrangements. Will you." He looked away from Priskin, which was the code for him to leave and to get on with it.

Chapter 9

As soon as he walked out of the front door Priskin got onto his smart phone. This is what he did for a living. He broke into strangers' homes and arranged for prostitutes to be around to perform sexual favours for Asamovich and his 'friends'. He hated it, but he was paid well. He had to do it. If he didn't do it someone else would. He called Monica and asked her to be here on Friday night at ten o'clock and to bring three girls with her. All had to be young. All had to be blonde. All had to be slim. And all had to agree to suck some stranger's penis. They would be well paid if they satisfied the gentlemen and stayed with them until breakfast. Sixteen thousand pounds was the agreed price. Four thousand pounds for each girl, for just ten hours work.

Following the meeting with the boss Priskin went home to Notting Hill. The cat was still in the kitchen. Andre was home early from school. He had a length of ribbon from his mum's work basket and was playing with the cat, driving it crazy by dangling the ribbon two inches from its face. Olga had been to a local supermarket to purchase tins of cat food, treats and water. She was not pleased that the cat was in the house but pleased for Andre who was enjoying playing with such an energic pet. It didn't look as if the novelty would end any time soon.

The Harrods' bag containing the collar were still in the back of his car, hidden under a blanket. He had to remove the bag before Olga found it and the collar and made the connections. She may already have had her doubts about the story of finding the cat outside on the street. It didn't seem feasible. If the cat was from the local area, why hadn't they seen it before? Of course, there were legitimate reasons why that may have been the case. Nonetheless, he knew he had to get rid of the bag and the collar and to return the cat to its rightful owner. He was going to let Andre enjoy playing with it for now. He was bound to lose interest before too long.

On Friday afternoon, Priskin took Olga shopping to the Westfield centre in Shepherd's Bush. He drove there and back in the 4x4. He had put the Harrods' bag and the collar into the space where the spare wheel was stored. It was extremely unlikely that she would find it there. Later in the afternoon they went into St John's Wood to collect Andre from school. It was a lazy day, for not doing a great deal.

After an evening meal, Priskin went into his study. He called Monica and asked her to arrive outside of the gates leading to Asamovich's home at ten. She said she would be there with three other girls. Two other Ukrainians and beautiful Romanian girl called Bella, who she said was a model. Asamovich liked tall and blonde girls from east European stock. They had to be slim. He disliked girls with excess weight, brunettes, or redheads. They had to be clean and free from STDs. He had a penchant for petite blondes with trim figures, small boobs, twenty to twenty-eight-years-of-age. If the girl loved kinky sex all the better. Priskin told Monica he would meet her at the gate in his car and drive them the hundred yards to the house. He would take them inside and into the conservatory, then leave them to it.

It was nine-thirty in the evening when Priskin drove from Notting Hill to Knightsbridge. On reaching the black iron gate he turned into the inlet. He had to pull up adjacent to the box in which a security guard was sitting on high stool. He nodded to the guy who opened the gate for him to drive onto the cobbled road, then up the road to the front of the mansion. He was there at close to ten to ten.

Lights were on in the upper floors. Asamovich's Bentley was parked on the pebble stone forecourt. Hector must have driven it to Heathrow Airport to collect Asamovich's friends, then brought them back here. Overhead the sky was starry. The cloudless sky meant it was chilly. The craters on the moon's surface were like smears of dust on a bright lightbulb. Leaves from the trees and shrubs were laid in the gutter. The rain of the past couple of days had left them mushy, the gutters blocked and therefore waterlogged.

Priskin didn't get out of his car. He was waiting for a few minutes, then at five to ten, he drove back up to the gate, pulled up, got out of the car, and stepped to the security box. He knew the chap in there by name. He had spoken to him before on numerous occasions mainly about football. His name was Jeff. He was an ex Met police officer. Jeff asked him what he could for him.

Priskin said he was meeting a group of people who he was expecting in the next few minutes. He would drive them the short distance to the mansion. Jeff said okay, not a problem. He asked Priskin if he had watched the football on the TV last night. Priskin said he hadn't.

Jeff knew the score. He had logged Hector leaving in the Bentley at noon, then recorded him coming back at four o'clock with three men inside. Then an hour later a van from Fortnum and Mason containing several hampers of food and drink arrived. It was no secret that a gathering of some kind was taking place in Asamovich's home. It wouldn't be the first. It wouldn't be the last.

It was dead on ten o'clock when a black cab pulled up outside the gate. The vehicle stopped, the back doors opened, and four young women climbed out. Priskin stepped through the gate and went to the driver's side of the cab. He handed him thirty pounds and told him to keep the change.

He joined the girls by the open gate. Monica was a trim, cute blonde with long muscly legs, a trim figure and agreeable looks. Her friends were just as pretty and shapely. Priskin took the ladies to his car to drive them the hundred yards to the house. He was soon at the gate, operating the opening device and driving onto the property. He parked his Kia by the Bentley, got out and led the four of them down the path to where the Russian flag was hanging limp on the pole by the entrance.

He showed the girls into the reception room, through a door then down a corridor and into the conservatory where the party would be commencing shortly. Several tables, which had food on them, had been erected by Mrs Andropov. Bottles of champagne were cooling in ice buckets. Easy listening pop music was playing out of the high speakers on the floor. The party would probably last a couple of hours, then each of the men would be invited to choose a girl of his choice to take to his room. The party would end at breakfast time. The girls would leave the house in a car driven by Priskin to a location of their choice. It was the same as before. Monica knew the set-up. She would have told her colleagues what to expect. It wasn't the first time for her. Although they weren't in the room, Priskin thought he knew who two of the men were. He didn't know the third one.

After managing the arrival of the call-girls and pouring them each a glass of the best cava, Priskin left the house. Rather than turn left out of the gate and go home, he decided to turn right and head in a different direction. He was heading into Brompton, then into Chelsea and onto Oakley Street.

He was soon on Brompton Road. Chelsea was just on the other side of the Kings Road. Once on Oakley Street, the area around

Dorset Gardens wasn't far away. It had been less than forty-eight hours since the break-in. A strange break-in, in many respects, because nothing had been taken. If it wasn't for the patio door been forced, the residents wouldn't know anyone had been in.

The cat's disappearance might be slightly more difficult to explain away. At the bottom end of Oakey Street there was a free parking space just around the corner from an Italian eatery on Kings Road, so he pulled in there. He went into the Italian place. It was a restaurant with a take-away counter. He ordered and paid for a Spaghetti Bolognese, telling the assistant he would be back to collect his meal in five minutes. He came out of the eatery and walked up Oakley Street towards the pillars of Albert Bridge in the distance. Three quarters of the way along the street he turned into the private road at Dorset Gardens. Residents' cars were parked in front of the big executive houses.

The pale sandstone clad facades were visible in the dark of the evening. The bulbs in the replica lampposts were dim. Illumination in the windows shone behind the Laura Ashley curtains and the plush venetian blinds. He carried on along the path, passed the end of the mews road where he had scurried down that morning. There was no evidence of a police presence. He carried on and came to the wrought iron rail fence at number forty-eight. There were no lights on in the windows. It was in dark. As soon as he was passed the house he turned back and walked back to the end of the street and back onto Oakley Street, then turned onto Kings Road. He went back into the Italian to collect his meal.

He drove home from there. When he arrived home, he put the dish into the oven to warm it, then he went into the lounge. The time was close to eleven o'clock. He didn't expect Olga to be up, but she was. The cat was sitting in her lap, literally lapping up the attention. It looked at home. Maybe he wouldn't be returning the animal to forty-eight Dorset Gardens, any time soon.

Chapter 10

The next morning was Saturday, which usually began with a lie-in until around nine, but today Priskin had to be at Asamovich's home for nine o'clock to collect the call-girls, pay Monica, then get them out of the house as quickly and as seamlessly as possible. He hoped, no he prayed, that he didn't need to do anything else, like hide a dead body or contact the emergency services to ask for an ambulance. He hated doing these tasks for his boss, covering up after him. Smoothing things out. Sorting out a mess. It was a strange relationship, though he very rarely thought about it. That would have depressed him even more.

It just so happened that Andre went to school on every third Saturday morning in the month to attend a kid's club. Little doubt, that he would be telling his school friends, those who already didn't know, that he had a cat. His mum had named the animal, 'Purrfect'.

It was ten past eight when Priskin put Andre into the car and set out for St John's Wood. It was half past eight when he pulled up outside the school. He took his son inside and into the classroom. The club was nothing more than a smart name for extra tuition. Andre's reading and writing were above the standard for a seven-year-old, but his Maths wasn't. He had to put in a little bit more time and effort to grasp the concepts, therefore he attended a morning club every third Saturday in the month.

The morning was cool. The sun was bright, but it provided little in the way of warmth. Once he had seen Andre into the classroom he left to drive across town to Knightsbridge. He was finding he was using his car more than usual these days. He vowed to return to using cabs as soon as possible.

He entered the house just before nine and went into the kitchen. Used plates and pots were piled high on the table in the centre of the room. Mrs Andropov was feeding them into a dishwasher. Uneaten food was on another table, along with at least two dozen empty bottles of Dom Perignon.

Mrs Andropov didn't say anything to Priskin, other than a courteous good morning. The look of disgust on her face at all of this waste said it all. Priskin gave her a forced smile. He couldn't do anything else. From the kitchen he went into the reception area where Monica and the other three girls were sitting around in chairs that had been taken out of the conservatory. He did a quick headcount to ensure there were four of them. Thankfully, there were four. Each one had the shoulder bag they had brought with them. They were quiet and exhausted. It must have been some party. Two of the girls looked worse for wear, from too much champagne poured down their throats, by the lecherous old fools who had used them for their sexual gratification. Monica and other one looked okay. He was relieved that he hadn't found a dead body in a bed.

There were no pools of blood to clear up or any other nasty surprises.

Monica looked at Priskin as he entered the room. "You have money. No?" she asked in her schoolgirl English. Her voice sounded as hoarse as sandpaper.

He withdrew two opaque cellophane packets from his jacket pocket and handed them to her. Each packet contained eight thousand pounds in banknotes. She took them from him and put them straight into her shoulder bag. He wanted them out of the house, sooner rather than later so he suggested he take them to his car. He would take them to a location of their choice. He was soon escorting the girls out of the house and into his car.

Now he was a taxi service for four call-girls. He didn't mind. It was all good fun. He dropped them off on Edgeware Road, outside a café that was frequented by east European escorts. They were happy. He was happy. It was the weekend, a time to relax with his wife and son.

The weather wasn't too bad for the beginning of October. Dimitri and Olga went supermarket shopping with Andre during the afternoon. Father and son kicked a football in the back garden until it got too dim to see and too chilly to stand around. That evening Priskin brought a family meal from a local eatery. It was very rare for them to do this, but it didn't hurt every now and again.

On Sunday morning, Priskin set out from his home on the premise of taking Andre to Regents Park. He told Olga they were going to go on the rowing boats on the Serpentine, then kick a football around. However, as they got into the car he had a change of mind. He headed south and set off to cross the Thames at Albert Bridge and visit Battersea park instead.

Once there. They went into the children's zoo and spent a couple of hours until it became too dark at four o'clock. On the way back over the river Priskin stopped along Oakley Street. He told Andre to stay in the car. He was just going for a short walk. He parked close to the top of the street, then walked down the length of the road towards the bridge end. He was close to the turn in to Dorset Gardens when his eyes caught sight of the notice attached to a lamppost. He went to it and read what was written on the card. It said:

'*MISSING CAT,*' then '*HAVE YOU SEEN THIS CAT?*'
There was a picture of 'Purrfect'. *The notice said 'Missing from 48 Dorset Gardens for three days. A Russian Blue called Sasha. Reward for information. Please call*'

Beneath the words were two telephone numbers. One a landline. The other one was a mobile. He took out his smart phone and tapped the landline number into the memory. It was probably the same number on the collar. From here he carried on over the turn in to Dorset Gardens to the first lamppost on the other side. The same notice was attached to it.

He walked back to his car, opened the door, and got into the driver's seat. Andre had fallen asleep in the ten minutes Priskin was out of the vehicle. He drove home. He didn't tell Olga what he had seen on the lamppost.

On Monday morning, Olga took Andre to school. Priskin spent the morning in the study browsing the internet on his PC. He was contemplating his next move. He felt awful. He knew he had to return the cat to its rightful owners shortly. He didn't want to call the number too soon. He knew that if he did there was no guarantee that he would speak to Dale Farthing. An assistant, a cleaner, a home-help or an au-pair might have posted the notice on the lamppost. Maybe, the Farthings were away on vacation. The possible connection to Saint Petersburg still intrigued him. As for the cat, Olga was beginning to voice one or two misgivings about keeping 'Purrfect'. She had complained about the amount of fur she was finding on the sofa and the armchairs, and the cost of feeding the animal. She had enquired about taking him to a vet to get him checked out. That could cost anything up to two hundred pounds. Money, they had, but why spend it if they planned to return it to its rightful owner? Olga said she would hate herself forever if 'Purrfect' was a child's pet. Andre was continuing to play with him and drive him mad by dangling a piece of ribbon in his face. Losing him would make him distraught, but he would get over it.

Priskin had an idea. He searched the internet for a local Chelsea free newspaper. He found an on-line reference for the 'Kensington and Chelsea Times'. He clicked on it. The pages of the newspaper popped up. He looked through the pages. There were no items about a burglary in Dorset Gardens. Maybe, it was too early. But today was Monday. It had been five days ago. He turned his PC off, then went into the kitchen to make himself a sandwich for lunch. He was going to collect Andre later. Olga was out until around five. She was meeting some friends in a 'ladies only' gym. Then she and some of her friends would go to a little Bistro in Hampstead for something to eat. She had a good mix of friends, mostly Brits, but a few Russians. She would have two hours on the treadmills, the weight machines, then a sauna, then retreat to the bistro for lunch and a chat with her friends.

From his study Priskin opened the door to the kitchen and looked inside. 'Purrfect' was sitting by the backdoor, looking at it, as if he wanted to go out. He had done his business in the litter tray. He turned to look at Priskin and give him a sad look. It was as if he was saying. 'Let me out, I want to find my way home'. Priskin decided at that moment to call the telephone number and set in motion the return of 'Purrfect' to his rightful owner. He closed the kitchen door, then went back into the study to get his phone with the telephone number in it. He sat in the black leather office chair, found the number, and called it, then he sat back and put the phone onto loudspeaker.

The dialling tone sounded for two minutes. He was about to terminate the call when a voice came on and said: "Hello. Who is it?" It was a male voice, strong and clear

"Hi," said Priskin. "I understand you've lost a cat."

"That's correct," said the man swiftly.

"Is it a grey cat with green-blue eyes?"

"Yes. A Russian Blue," he replied. He didn't sound like the home help. He had a strong and crisp posh accent. "Do you have him?" he asked in hope.

"I think so," said Priskin.

"Oh my God. Where did you find him?"

"I found a cat outside of my house. I live in Notting Hill," said Priskin.

"Notting Hill! Oh, my word," said the man, with an emotional edge in his voice.

Priskin continued. "I went out on Thursday morning and heard the sound of a cat making a meow sound. When I looked on the path I got the shock of my life. There was a cat sitting on the path. I'd never seen it before. I brought it into the house, so it could get warm."

"Thank you," said the man. Even though their conversation was short Priskin could see a man in his mid-thirties to early-forties in his mind's eye. He sounded polished and well educated. London born and bred. It seemed to tie in with the image of the home and the man he had briefly seen at the auction, ten days ago. It must have been Dale Farthing on the other end of the telephone.

"Are you able to return him?" the man asked.

"Of course," said Priskin. "What's your address?" he asked.

"Forty-eight. Dorset Gardens in Chelsea. We're just off Oakley Street."

"Okay. I think I know it," said Priskin.

"If you come down Oakley Street, we're about two thirds of the way down towards the bridge. It's on a private road," the man said.

"I'll find it," said Priskin.

"How did you know to call this number?" the man asked.

"Coincidence really," said Priskin, off the top of his head. The man didn't respond. He was waiting for him to continue. Priskin had a second to think. "A friend came to my home earlier today. He lives in that area. I showed him the cat. He said there are some notices not far from him about a missing cat in Chelsea. I thought geez what are the chances of that. Must be a thousand to one."

"I'd say," said the man.

"So, I drove there and sure enough there are the notices. I could see it's the same cat. What's your name?" Priskin asked.

"My name?"

"Yes."

"Dale Farthing."

"Is nice to talk to you Mr Farthing."

"And who are you?" Farthing asked.

"Me?"

"Yes."

"I'm Dimitri. Dimitri Priskin from Notting Hill."

"Nice of you to call Mr Priskin. Your call comes as a delightful surprise. We thought we'd lost him forever."

"We?"

"My wife Octavia and I," Farthing replied.

"I have to collect my son later today from his school in St John's Wood," said Priskin. "Is it okay if I call around this evening at about six?" he asked.

"Absolutely," said Farthing. "Thank you, very much."

"No. Don't thank me," said Priskin. "It's my delight."

"There's a reward," said Farthing.

"I don't require a reward," said Priskin. "My reward is returning the cat to his home. I'm so pleased I've been able to track down the owner so soon. He's such a lovely cat. Very affectionate."

"Yes, he is. I look forward to meeting you later," Farthing said.

"Likewise," said Priskin.

"Bye for now," said Farthing.

"Bye," said Priskin. He ended the call, then he spent the next two minutes reflecting on the conversation. The man, Dale Farthing, now had his mobile phone number. Had he made a colossal mistake calling him? Possibly. But he thought the conversation had gone well. Maybe better than he expected. The line about finding the cat on the path outside his house did sound plausible. Things like that do happen. Farthing hadn't mentioned anything about a break-in. Overall, Priskin thought it had gone okay. He got up from the table and glanced at the clock on the wall above the desk. The time was getting on for three o'clock. Olga would be home at five. She would be pleased that the cat was going home.

At twenty to four Priskin left home en-route to collect Andre from school. Before leaving he left a written note on a cork board in the kitchen, they used for messages. It was to tell Olga, if she came home early, that he had spoken to the cat's owner and that he would be returning 'Purrfect' to his rightful home this evening. He made sure the kitchen door was closed, then he left the house.

Chapter 11

On the way home from St John's Wood, Priskin had the task of telling his son that 'Purrfect' would be going home this evening because his owner wanted him back. He promised Andre that, if his mum agreed, they would all pay a visit to a local pet store and he could choose a cat of his own. Andre played the part of the little, old solider. He didn't cry though his bottom lip did begin to tremble. In defiance, he said he didn't want a cat, he wanted a doggie instead. Priskin had to smile to himself.

On arriving home, they found Olga in the kitchen preparing the evening meal. She had come home early. She had read the note Dimitri had left her.

"How did you trace the owner?" she asked.

"You won't believe this," he said. She didn't reply. "I was driving along Kings Road on a job for Asamovich. I saw a notice on a lamppost. It was near to that Italian restaurant we've been in. I stopped and had a look. It was asking for information about a missing cat. I took a note of the telephone number and called it this afternoon."

She still didn't reply. Maybe she did believe him, maybe she didn't. Before she could interrogate him further the alarm on the oven sounded. The salmon was ready to take out. The new potatoes were bubbling in the pan on the hob and the salad had been washed.

After the evening meal was over, it was time for Priskin to take 'Purrfect' home. Olga picked him up and gave his fur one last long lingering stroke. The cat closed his eyes tight and purred. She passed him to her husband. Andre was still sitting at the dining table with a fork in his hand. He was being brave. He held a tear back. Over dinner his mum promised him they would consider buying him a puppy for his eight birthday which was only a month away.

Priskin held 'Purrfect' tight. He took him out to his car, opened the back door and put him on the back seat. Once he was safely inside, he climbed into the front, got the motor running and pulled away from the front of his house. He considered what to do about the Harrods' bag, then decided to leave it for now.

He was soon passing going through Brompton and turning onto the Kings Road. After two hundred yards he turned right onto Oakley Street and drove at a restrained pace to the bottom end. It had been five days since the break-in. He wondered if he would be met not only by Dale Farthing, but the police as well, wanting to ask him if he was responsible for the break-in. Suddenly, he felt a little on edge, but determined to return the animal come-what-may. He would have to blag his way through it. He liked the word 'blag'. It was one of his favourite English words, though he didn't know its origin or anything like that.

Despite the sound of the traffic, he could, at times, hear the cat meowing. After a few hundred yards he turned left off Oakley Street and into the narrow inlet of the private road. He drove up the cobbled terrain to the front of number forty-eight and pulled up right in front of the wrought iron fence. There were lights on in the downstairs window to the right of the front door. The retro streetlights reflected in the double-pane glass in the wide window. The blinds over the windows in the first-floor rooms were down. The shrubs in the garden were still in a non-existent breeze. At three minutes past six in the second week of October, the last trace of sunlight had disappeared from the sky in the past ten minutes. As the sun dropped what warmth there was had gone with it. It was a night for fleeces, woolly hats, and mittens.

Priskin killed the engine, got out of the vehicle, then opened the back door. 'Purrfect' seemed to know where he was. He gave a little whimper as Priskin took hold of him and held him close to his chest. "You're going home," he said as if the cat would understand his every word.

He held him with both hands, then closed the door with his foot, stepped across the pavement, opened the gate in the fence and moved down the path to the front door.

At the door he pressed the doorbell and waited. A light appeared in the heart shaped glass panel in the door. Within a matter of seconds, the door came open and standing there in the door frame wasn't a man, but a very attractive dark-haired woman in her mid-thirties. She must have been five-nine tall. She was wearing a grey turtle neck sweater and rose-coloured cord pants that were tight around her thighs. She had diamond studs in the lobes of both ears

94

and an African gold plate bangle around her left wrist. She was pencil slim, had nice boobs and a curvy figure. On seeing the cat, she let out a squeal of delight, reached out and grabbed him from Priskin's arms.

"Oh, my Sasha. Oh, my Sasha," she said twice. A man appeared in the hallway and came to stand close behind her. He placed his hands on her shoulders, then he looked at Priskin. "Please come in," he said. Priskin assumed he was the man he had spoken to on the telephone. He had a head of thick grey hair, but he wasn't elderly. He was perhaps in his early-to-mid-forties. He was wearing drainpipe style jeans and a burgundy cardigan, over a polo shirt. He was around five ten tall and just as slim as the woman. He was a handsome man with big eyes, trim eyebrows, thin lips, and a fine set of teeth. On first impression he looked like the man who had purchased the Faberge eggs at the auction.

Priskin stepped into the house and glanced around the interior. He was seeing the interior in electric light, not in the featureless drab of the early morning hours. The lady put her lips to the top of Sasha's head and gave him a kiss.

"Sasha. Where have you been?" she asked.

'Sasha,' thought Priskin. He much preferred 'Purrfect'.

Dale Farthing looked at Priskin. "You don't know how much we've missed him. We're so pleased to have him back."

The attractive brunette raised her eyes to Priskin. "It's been agony for us," she said. She was almost crying with joy. Priskin detected an accent. She smiled. Her perfect face radiated warmth. Her deep-set eyes were walnut brown.

"How did you find him?" she asked. Her accent did have a slight east European edge to it.

"I didn't tell my wife about our conversation. I left it as a surprise," said the man.

"Oh right. Okay," said Priskin responding to his words. It was in some ways a nasty thing to do, but in another quite sweet. He couldn't make up his mind which it was. He directed his eyes on the lady. "I live in Notting Hill," he said. "I found Sasha sitting on the path outside of my home on Thursday morning. I thought it was strange. I was going to alert the local cats protection people. It was so cold I brought him into my house and put him in the kitchen by the heater, so he could be warm."

"Thank you very much," she said. She put her lips on the cat's head for a second time and gave him another kiss. Sasha responded by purring out loud and tightly closing his eyes.

"Please come through into the sitting-room," said Farthing.

At the doorway into the room he gestured to an armchair that backed onto the long window with a view onto the front garden. "Please take a seat. Can I get you anything to drink?"

"No thank you," said Priskin. "I'm driving."

"Fine," said Farthing. "By the way my name is Dale Farthing. This is my wife Octavia."

"Dimitri Priskin," replied Priskin smiling.

Priskin sat in the chair, snuggled into the cushion, and crossed his legs. The room was illuminated by light from a tall, thin stemmed silver coated lampstand. In the illumination the room looked fundamentally different than it did in the dark. It was far cosier. Far less sterile than he recalled. There were rich fabrics, expensive wallcoverings, plenty of colour and panache and the lovely fragrance of a lady's perfume. The effect was like an interior designers wet-dream. It had the stamp of originality.

Farthing looked to Priskin. "Did you say your name is Dimitri?"

"That's correct."

"It sounds Russian. Is there a family connection?" Farthing asked.

"My father was Russian. My mother is English"

Farthing noticed the word 'was'. "Was?" he asked inquisitively.

"My father passed away several years ago," Priskin replied.

"I'm sorry to hear that. Octavia was born in St Petersburg."

"No way," said Priskin. "It's a small world. My wife was born in St Petersburg. I was born and raised in Moscow."

Octavia Farthing came into the room. She was no longer holding Sasha.

"You won't believe this," said Farthing to her. "Dimitri was born in Moscow. His wife is a native of St Petersburg."

"Oh, my word," she said. She smiled, then ran a hand through her long hair. She was a very attractive lady with the poise and the strut of a diva. Her corduroy trousers showed off her slim thighs and trim backside. Priskin's eyes went to the picture frame above the fireplace. There was the painting. The Monet style impression of the Winter Palace in St Petersburg with what must have been snow on the ground and on the rooftops.

"Is that the Winter Palace?" he asked. "I had a similar picture to that in my parents' home when I was a child."

"You don't say?" said Farthing.

"What do you do?" asked Octavia, suddenly changing the subject.

"Pardon me."

"For a livelihood?" she clarified.

"I work in Finance for a single client with a fortune to manage," Priskin replied. He glanced to Farthing. "How about you?" he asked.

Farthing suddenly looked ill at ease for some reason. He shrugged his shoulders. Priskin thought this indicated that they were independently wealthy and didn't need to work to survive comfortably. Maybe he had, as the British say, being born with a silver spoon in his mouth. Husband and wife choose not to reveal too much to a stranger. Farthing recovered his composure. He eyed Priskin. A sudden thought appeared before Priskin. Maybe Farthing recognised him from the auction. But he had been sitting at the back of the hall behind Farthing, and the room was packed. He didn't see him turn around to look back so maybe he didn't recognise him. As soon as the bidding had come to a stop Priskin had left by the back exit. Farthing was still taking congratulations from the people around him. Neither of them had said a word during the bidding, so he wouldn't recognise his voice.

Octavia took a step to a side and sat on the arm rest next to her husband. He wrapped an arm around her waist and squeezed her tight.

"Where in Moscow did you live?" she asked. Maybe she was testing him, thought Priskin. Maybe to see if he would be able to answer the question.

"From the age of five months up to seventeen I lived in my parent's apartment on Leninsky Avenue, close to Gorky Park."

"How long have you lived in London?" she asked.

"Close to fourteen years," he replied.

"How about yourself?" Priskin asked looking at Octavia.

"Eighteen years. I came to England with my father and mother." She was about to say something else but changed tact. She moved her legs to a side. "What's your wife's name?" she asked.

"Olga. Olga Patrovski is her name," he replied.

"How long have you lived in Notting Hill?" Farthing asked.

"Coming up for nine years."

"Do you have a family?" she asked.

"A son aged seven. Andre."

"So, you're in Finance?" Farthing asked. "Who do you work for?"

"A wealthy individual client," he replied without naming Asamovich.

"Sounds intriguing," replied Farthing.

"I manage my client's money and stock holdings. That kind of thing," was Priskin's vague reply. "How long have you lived here?" he asked changing the subject.

He still couldn't get over how pretty Octavia was. She had smooth skin and exquisite colouring. Her long dark hair shimmered in the incoming light to reveal the trace of a purple tint. The turtle neck sweater hugged her figure. She was far prettier and easier on the eye than Olga.

"We've lived here for two years," said Farthing.

"But we're thinking of leaving," she added.

"Why's that?" Priskin asked.

"We don't feel safe in this part of the city any longer," Dale Farthing said.

"We're just getting over a break in," she said.

Priskin didn't move a millimetre. He kept his legs crossed and his eyes and expression fixed.

"That's awful," he said. They didn't reply. "When was it? Was anything taken?" he asked.

"That's the strange thing," said Farthing. "Nothing was taken. The only thing we lost was Sasha. Other than Sasha nothing else of value."

"Sentimental value?" Priskin asked.

"Sorry," said Dale Farthing. He either didn't hear the question or he was being bumptious.

"You said, other than Sasha. Nothing of value."

Octavia cleared her throat. "Sasha is a pure bred Russian Blue. He's worth a small fortune. At least twenty-five thousand pounds," she said.

Priskin was stunned. "Good grief," he said. He sounded so English it was uncanny. He put it down to watching all those dramas on TV.

"The people who broke into the house may not have known Sasha's value," added Farthing to emphasis his wife's words.

"That figures," said Priskin. "And they left him in Notting Hill for some reason," he added.

"Who can guess?" said Farthing. He ran a hand through his mop of grey hair. He was a distinguished man, eloquent, though Priskin detected that he may have harboured an edge. There may have been a backstory to him, one that was not wholly pleasant. His accent suggested that he was not from the London area.

"Are you from London?" Priskin asked him.

"Me?" Farthing asked. "No, I was born in Norfolk. My family are in pig farming. I came to London twenty years ago to work in Marketing. That's how I met my wife," he said.

"Norfolk?" Priskin asked.

"Yes. Just north of Norwich. I've still got a little bit of a Norfolk accent."

"I like it," said Octavia.

She put her hand on his shoulder and patted him on the head as if she was patting a small dog. There was a period of silence which seemed to last longer than it should have done. Priskin made to get up from the chair. As he pushed himself up he glanced back to look out of the front window onto the street where his vehicle was visible through the gaps inbetween the wrought iron railing.

Dale Farthing got up out of his seat. "Thank you for returning Sasha to us. We feared we'd never see him again. The police said there have been some burglaries in the area and a lot of attempts. We may have been lucky. Whoever came in decided to take the cat. Lucky for us they didn't know his value," he said.

"Quite incredible," said Priskin. It was a phrase he had never used before in his life.

"One moment," said Octavia suddenly. Priskin was put on alert. "What are you doing on Saturday evening?" she asked.

"Not sure," Priskin replied.

"We're entertaining some friends at a small dinner party. Nothing special. It's a jeans and t-shirt event. We'd be delighted if you and your wife could join us. We usually have pizza and a few other snacks," she said.

Priskin got to his feet. "That's very kind of you," he said. "What time?" he asked.

"Let's say about eight-thirty," she said.

"I'll inform my wife. I'm sure she'll be delighted to meet you," Priskin said. He could hardly say no. They may have suspected that it was him who had stolen Sasha, but there was no obvious indication that that was the case.

"That's great," said Farthing. "I'll show you out," he added.

Priskin said goodbye to Octavia, then Dale showed him into the hallway and on to the front door. He opened it and let him out into the cold night air. They shook hands, then Priskin was away. He had to go home to inform Olga that they would be going out on Saturday evening to a 'jeans and t-shirt' dinner party. Whatever, 'jeans and t-shirt' meant.

As he got into his car, he couldn't help but think that he had seen Octavia Farthing before. But he couldn't place where.

Chapter 12

Olga said she would be delighted to meet the Farthings. She said she would need to buy a new frock for the occasion. When Dimitri told her, it was a 'jeans and t-shirt' party she was a little disappointed, but still thrilled that she would be meeting new people, one of whom was from her home city. She was also pleased that the cat was now back with its loving owners.

Priskin asked her if she knew anyone called Octavia. He described her as a tall, dark-haired lady who looked moneyed. Olga said that the only Octavia she had heard of was the daughter of a man by the name of Sergei Molinsky. But that she didn't know her personally.

Molinsky was one of the original Russian rich who had made his home in London. Priskin wondered if Octavia Farthing could be his daughter? It was a possibility, but not a definite. If there was a connection, then Priskin considered the possibility that Dale Farthing had purchased the Faberge eggs on Molinsky's behalf. Molinsky was known to be an avid collector of Russian artefacts like eggs and works of art. Molinsky was worth far more than Yuri Asamovich's two-hundred-million-pound fortune. Five hundred and sixty thousand pounds was not a lot of money to him.

Saturday evening came. Olga took Andre to stay the night with a neighbour. He was good friends with their eight-year-old son, Jackson, with whom Andre played in a local park.

The Priskin's arrived at the Farthing home at eight-thirty on the dot. They had heeded Octavia's advice about the party attire. Olga had squeezed into an old pair of Levi 505's. She had put on a short-sleeved blouse. Dimitri was wearing a pair of slim fit jeans and a blue round neck t-shirt with a well-known sports logo plastered on the front.

There were no cars parked outside of number forty-eight Dorset Gardens by the time they arrived. A Mercedes convertible was in the drive by the side of the house that led to the garage. The evening was very similar to the previous visit to the house. There was a hint of mist in the air and a scent of autumn. The mist was probably coming from the wide stretch of the Thames which was less than a quarter of a mile away. The sky was starry, so it was rather chilly. A firework exploded somewhere close by. The 5th of November was only a couple of weeks away.

Priskin led his wife up the garden path to the front door. He was carrying a bottle of expensive wine he had purchased from a wine store on the Kings Road, as a gift for the Farthings. He knocked once on the solid wood. The door opened almost immediately and there was a beaming Dale Farthing.

"Welcome. Come in," he said. His eyes went to Olga to give her the once over. Olga was attractive, but she wasn't in Octavia's league. Olga was well turned out, but didn't have Octavia's shapely legs, figure or clear unblemished skin. Still she was a lot more stylish than many British women her age.

Priskin held out the bottle of wine he had in his hand for Farthing. He took it and looked at the label. It wasn't very expensive, but it was a nice vintage.

"Nice," he said, then. "Thanks." He meant it.

From the hallway, Farthing led them into the dining room at the rear of the house. It looked out on the decking close to the patio area and the back garden which was partially floodlit by a security light that must have been added since the door had been forced.

A flame fire inserted into the wall provided a warm glow. The central dining table was set with plates, cutlery, and several types of drinking vessels. Candles burned in glass pots. Round lights inserted into the ceiling provided a low intimate light, which when combined with the flames from the candles gave the room a shadowy cosy feel. In the background, a medley of Katie Melua tracks were playing at low volume. On a table at the other side of the room there was food in glass bowls and on plates. There were numerous nibbles: samosas, black and green olives, salad, cheese and crackers, pickles, sausages on sticks, various cold meats, and slices of baked homemade pizza. The easy listening music provided the cultural back drop.

Just then the door that led into the kitchen opened and Octavia emerged with four other people. Two couples of similar age to the Priskin's. Octavia introduced them to Dimitri and Olga. They were Paul and Melissa Saunders, and John and Carla Redmond. They were friends and near neighbours of the Farthings. Both couples were wearing similar casual dress. Octavia went back into the kitchen, whilst Dale began some chit-chat. It was all very civilised and adult.

Octavia soon returned into the dining room carrying a large punch bowl that was three quarters full of liquid. She put it down carefully on the dining table then placed a ladle in it.

It wasn't going to be so much a dinner party, but a relaxing, alcoholic fuelled night between eight adults. All eight of them each took a plate and went to the buffet table to pick food from the wide selection. Dimitri chose a slice of pizza, some cheese, and olives. It was nice and relaxing, and everyone was gracious and friendly. Octavia took the ladle and poured everyone a healthy amount of the punch. Then they sat around the table and the chit-chat soon began. Dale Farthing introduced Dimitri to his friends as 'the man who had returned Sasha to them', therefore, he was a bit of a hero.

John Redmond was an investment banker with his own business so Priskin and he got on fine talking about the financial markets. The Saunders were both dentists who had their own private practice in Chelsea, Hampstead, and South Kensington. They were all professional people, well educated, sophisticated, and wealthy.

By nine-thirty the mood music had changed. It was now far grittier and dominated by several mainstream light-rock tracks. Priskin had drunk a couple of large glasses of the punch so he was already feeling a little light-headed and bleary-eyed.

John Redmond was an all right kind of guy. For an investment banker he wasn't full of his own self-importance or financial acumen. Priskin told him that he worked for a single rich client.

"Tell me Dimitri," Redmond said. "Who is the rich client you work for?" he asked.

Priskin was in two minds whether to tell him when Olga suddenly blurted out. "He works for Yuri Asamovich."

Farthing looked at Priskin. "Yuri Asamovich?" he asked.

"Yuri Asamovich is my boss," Priskin confirmed.

"How do you come to be in London?" Redmond enquired.

Priskin sniffed. He suddenly felt a little exposed and light headed. The orange taste of the Cointreau in the punch repeated on him, not once but twice.

"My father, Anatoli was Russian. He passed away a few years ago. My mother is English. I was born in Moscow, thirty-three years ago." He didn't know why he had told them his age, but he had. "My parents divorced. My mother came back here to live in England. I followed her to London to attend university. I only intended to stay here for the duration of the course. Fourteen years later I'm still here."

"Are you thinking about returning to Moscow?" Paul Saunders asked him.

"We don't think so. Our son was born here and…" Olga said.

Priskin chipped in. "To pack up and go to Moscow would be too much of a wrench," he said.

"So how long have you known Yuri Asamovich?" Farthing asked.

"About nine years," he replied.

Octavia took the ladle in the bowl and poured everyone another round of punch. There was still a quarter remaining in the bowl.

"Not for me," said Priskin. "I'm driving."

"We can get a taxi," said Olga.

"That's right," said Farthing.

Although, he didn't want any more alcohol Priskin said okay. Octavia poured him another full glass.

Paul and Melissa Saunders left the party at ten-thirty. Olga and Octavia were engaged in chat about St Petersburg. They were reminiscing about their favourite places and growing up in the same city; that kind of thing. The three men were talking about politics then it turned to football. Dale Farthing said he had access to a hospitality box at Stamford Bridge, the home of Chelsea Football Club. He invited Priskin to join him and Redmond for a forthcoming match. Priskin said he would be delighted to attend. Farthing said his father-in-law would be attending.

"Who is your father-in-law?" Priskin asked.

"Sergei Molinsky," replied Farthing. "Do you know him?"

Priskin was right. Octavia Farthing was Sergei Molinsky's daughter. "I know him by name only. I've never met him," he replied.

"If you come to the game next Saturday. You'll meet him," said Farthing. He turned to his wife and asked her if she wanted coffee. She said okay. He went into the kitchen to prepare cups of fresh bean coffee.

By eleven o'clock the party had been going for two and a half hours. Priskin was feeling giddy from a combination of too much alcohol and too much food. John Redmond and his wife left at ten past eleven. Leaving the Farthings and the Priskins. A bond of friendship between Olga and Octavia was been established. The two ladies shared stories about growing up in St. Petersburg. They had even attended the same dance school and knew several of the teachers who had taught them. They compared life in Russia to that in England, which they said wasn't all that different, except London tended to be warmer in winter, but not by that much. The big difference was that Olga's father had been a relatively low-level official in the city council, whereas Octavia's father was Sergei Molinsky, who in his time in Russia was a government insider and an associate of no-less a figure than Vladimir Putin.

Sergei Molinsky had made millions of roubles in much the same way as Yuri Asamovich. He had acquired a state-owned industry at a knock-down price, then issued shares before floating them on the MICEX, the Moscow stock market. As the shares hit a high he sold them and made millions of dollars, which he put into Swiss bank accounts. He then purchased other businesses to widen his portfolio of interests, until he became worth one billon US dollars. Once he had made a billion he got out of Russia. His preferred destination was Switzerland, but he chose London because of the British Government's 'no questions, laissez-faire policy' towards rich Russians.

It was now more than obvious to Priskin that Farthing had purchased the eggs on behalf of his father-in-law to get around recently introduced laws that prevented such items falling into the hands of foreign nationals and leaving the United Kingdom.

Both the Priskins had had a few more glasses of the punch so they were well on the way to being inebriated. As promised Dale Farthing called them a cab at eleven-thirty. They were back home by midnight. They had had a good time and met some nice people, who might become firm friends in the future.

Chapter 13

Priskin woke up at ten o'clock with a thumping headache. Olga was already downstairs. He could hear her chastising Andre about something. It was the usual Sunday schedule. They would go for a walk in the afternoon, then he would watch some television with his son, whilst Olga did some clothes washing, then he recalled he had to go back to Dorset Gardens to collect his car. He laid in bed wide-awake. He had enjoyed last night and meeting Dale's friends. They were all good people. Well-to-do and successful. The food was simple, but nice, and the punch had tasted delightful for the first three samples, but not much after the next half a dozen.

He had had an inkling that Octavia Farthing was Sergei Molinsky's daughter and so it proved to be. It pointed to the likelihood that Farthing had purchased the Faberge eggs for his father-in-law.

After the brief lie-in was over he got out of bed and took a long hot shower, then he went downstairs. One hour later Dimitri, Olga and Andre went out for a walk into the centre of Notting Hill to visit a local coffee shop, where Priskin would browse through the Sunday morning newspapers for an hour.

Once they were back home Olga made sandwiches for lunch. Rather than call a taxi Priskin decided to walk the couple of miles or so into Chelsea to collect his car. Olga had said she would come with him, but Andre had fallen asleep on the sofa, so she decided to stay at home with him. It was at these times that Priskin wished they were a two-car family. Olga had made a conscious decision not to purchase a second car, because she wanted to do the right thing for the environment and reduce their carbon footprint. Anyway, Priskin knew he could do with the exercise. He hadn't played tennis or squash at the sports club for a while, so he needed to get out and get some exercise. He had to return to the club sometime soon. The walk to the Farthings home would sweat some of the alcohol out of his body. He hadn't figured on the amount of spirits that would be available at the party, nor its effect on him. Olga had also had a couple too many and blabbed to them about Yuri Asamovich. But still no harm done. It wasn't a threatening disclosure.

It was three o'clock when he set out to walk to Chelsea. It was the middle of October. The pathways were thick with fallen leaves from the trees. He had donned a heavy fleece jacket, a woolly beany hat, gloves, and a scarf.

By the time he reached the junction with Kings Road and Oakley Street he was glad he had put the warm clothes on. It took him forty-five minutes to reach Dorset Gardens, though this did include a stop at a supermarket for a cup of machine coffee.

His car was parked outside of the Farthing's home. The gate was open a few inches, so he stepped down the path to the front door. He had better see if they were in, so he could say thanks for last night. It would be rude of him to just drive away without at least calling.

The blinds in the upstairs rooms were down. Those in the downstairs hovered somewhere between up and down. He pressed the doorbell and waited in front of the blue door. The door opened and there was Dale Farthing in a chunky sweater and a pair of knee length cargo pants. The spectacles over his eyes were half on - half off his nose.

"Come in," he said. He took Priskin into the sitting-room. It looked as if he was home-alone. Octavia was nowhere to be seen. Priskin took a seat. The blue topped flames in the wall insert gas fire were twisting and sending out a lovely heat that had the room toast warm.

"Thanks for last night," Priskin said. "We really enjoyed it."

"Good," said Farthing…. "We aim to please," he added.

Priskin glanced around the room. There was an open, broadsheet Sunday morning newspaper spread across the sofa.

"Octavia is out with some friends," Farthing volunteered. "She meets them every Sunday afternoon. Tell me about Yuri Asamovich," he asked suddenly and unexpectedly. He didn't seem to want to waste much time with probing questions.

"There's nothing much to tell," said Priskin, picking his words carefully.

Farthing gave him a neutral look. He could perhaps sense that Priskin was treading carefully. "What's he like to work for?" he asked.

Priskin thought about his reply. After the cold of outside, the heat inside the house was powerful. He could feel his spine tingling with perspiration. "I think you'd say okay," he replied cautiously, but then for some inexplicable reason he changed tact. He sat back and stretched his legs out. "If you must know he's a bit of a rogue," he said.

"In what way?" Farthing asked.

"The usual," said Priskin.

Farthing shrugged his shoulders. "How?"

"Demanding," Priskin replied.

"In what way?" Farthing asked again.

"Wants things doing. Won't take no for an answer."

Farthing widened his eyes. "He sounds a lot like my father-in-law," he said tersely.

"Yuri wants a lot of things," said Priskin.

"Such has?" Farthing asked.

"Loyalty. But treats me like a lap dog. I think some people call it a go-for." Farthing smirked as if he knew exactly what he was saying. "You know about the European Union development fund?" Priskin asked.

"No. What is it?" Farthing asked.

"About twenty-five years ago the European Union gave a Russian development agency a gift of three hundred million dollars. The agency was supposed to cascade the money down to fund enterprise. The communists had just called time. The situation in the country was grave. To encourage swift economic development and integration the EU agreed to give the agency the money. The thing is most of the money was never used for the purpose it was supposed to be for. The agency was run by four men who kept the money and swindled the EU. The men disappeared with the money. One of those men was Yuri Asamovich."

"You're kidding?" said Farthing, sitting up. "Who are the other three?" he asked.

"I'm not sure who they are," Priskin replied.

"So, he's a wanted man?"

Priskin puckered his lips. "No. Not really."

"Why?"

"Because the EU wanted to keep it quiet. It was a secret transaction. However, one Russian investigator began to make enquiries and dig deeper. The EU didn't need the bad publicity and denied everything. The reporter stuck to the task. He discovered that

Asamovich may have had a hand in the disappearance of the money. In effect they had embezzled the Russian government by making multiple applications for assistance. But they were the same people. The reporter found the paper trail. He was going to make his findings public…"

"Was?" Farthing asked.

"Was. Until someone ordered his assassination. He was shot dead on a Moscow street."

Farthing's jaw dropped open. "What murdered?"

"By an unknown killer."

"Was Asamoivich involved in this?" he asked.

"That's the speculation," said Priskin.

"Oh, my word."

"That's how ruthless he can be," said Priskin. "Then he bid for Russian state-owned corporations and bought them with the money he embezzled out of the fund. Issued shares which he bought in their millions, then floated the companies on the stock market. He was the majority share-holder along with some of the others. The price of the shares shot-up in value when investors saw them as a sure-fire winner. He sold them on the market for up to one hundred times their initial value. Shares that may have been worth one dollar were worth one hundred dollars. He made a huge profit."

"How much?" Farthing asked.

"Probably about six hundred million US dollars. He had to pay off some corrupt government officials who had learned what had gone on. I reckon he spent around four hundred million in hush-money. But he still had a net value of two hundred million dollars."

"Where's the money?" Farthing asked.

"Most of it's in secret Swiss bank accounts."

"Who knows about his connection with the murder of the reporter?"

"It's probably common knowledge in Moscow." Priskin replied. "But there's no direct evidence," he added.

"No evidence?" Farthing asked in a tone that suggested he was in some ways disappointed, for a reason that was not obvious.

"No. Why would there be? They covered up their tracks well," said Priskin.

"Who knows about it here in the UK?"

"About what?"

"The whole episode with the European Union fund and the murder of the reporter," Farthing said.

"Some people in high circles might know," Priskin replied.

"But nothing's been done about it. Is that what you're saying?"

"The Russian government has never asked for his extradition back there. I'll assume from that they have no hard evidence to tie him to it. The British government are happy for people like him to be here," said Priskin.

"Much like Sergei," said Farthing.

"I know the name. But that's all I know about your father-in-law," said Priskin.

"What does Asamovich buy with his money?" Farthing asked.

"He buys works of art. He got a collection. Its only small. He's got a Gaugin, a Monet, a Van Gogh. He collects Russian art and valuable antiques. He's also got a vintage car collection."

"What about women?" Farthing asked.

"He's got a thing for east European prostitutes. Blondes mostly. He likes their fierce spirit." Farthing chuckled. "Tell me about Sergei Molinsky," Priskin asked.

Farthing paused to consider his words for a few moments "Not much different from Asamovich. Similar connections. He got involved with the development of the Russian stock market. He bought several companies. Purchased the shares. Floated the companies. Sold the shares on the open market and made a great deal of money. Then bought failing businesses throughout eastern Europe. Asset stripped and did deals. Then he dabbled in the arms trade. Bought arms on the open market and sold them through a Pakistani middleman to rouge states for huge profits," Farthing said.

"How much is he worth?"

"At current rates I'd say about three billion dollars US. Two billion sterling."

"Do you work for him?" Priskin asked.

He chose not to answer the question right away. He chewed on it for a few long moments. "No. Not much," he said. "The truth is that he's got several children through various relationships. He gives Octavia an annual allowance of one million pounds a year. She's his favourite."

A penny dropped through Priskin's head. Octavia had the money. Dale Farthing didn't have much to his name. He lived off his wife's money. The house. The fine furniture. The Maserati in the garage. The money in the bank. It all belonged to her. He was living on his wife's money. If she tied of him, he would have nothing. He was a good-looking guy and he had plenty of charm, but her eye could soon turn to another admirer. He must have been worried sick that she would leave him penniless.

"What does Molinsky do with his money?" Priskin asked.

"Much like Asamovich. He buys valuable things and stores them away. He collects Faberge eggs. He's got a collection second to none."

Priskin managed to stifle a cough. The door to the room opened wide and who should saunter into the room, but Sasha. Farthing looked at the cat, then put his eyes back on Priskin. Did he know that Priskin was the other bidder? He didn't say he did and there was no indication that he did know. The cat sauntered around the room, jumped onto the sofa, and snuggled into a cushion.

Priskin wanted to ask Farthing if he had any children with Octavia but elected not to ask the question. The cat could have been their only child through choice or for another reason.

"If you're coming to the football on Saturday. You'll meet Sergei," said Farthing.

"I wouldn't miss it for the world."

"Do you watch football?" Farthing asked.

"Not for a while. I watched CSKA now and again when I lived in Moscow. But not in London," he admitted.

"I follow Chelsea," said Farthing, as if he was proud of it and wanted to be associated with their success. "They've been my team since I was knee-high-to-a-grasshopper," he added.

Priskin smiled. He liked that phrase. He would bank it in his memory to use one day.

Just then the wrought iron gate leading onto the drive turned inward and a top-of-the-range Mercedes convertible appeared at the end of the driveway.

"Octavia is returning," said Farthing. "Stop and say hello."

"Of course," said Priskin. "I'll be delighted to." He watched as car came onto the forecourt and stopped. The driver's door opened, and she stepped out. She was elegant in a silver-grey trouser suit. Her swagger was like a cat-walk model. Her long dark hair flowed over the shoulders of the jacket that was nipped in at the waist. Farthing got to his feet.

"Do me a favour," he asked.

"Sure," said Priskin. "What is it?"

"Don't mention our conversation," he said.

"No, I won't," said Priskin. He wondered why he would ask him to do that. It suggested to him that they had secrets. They came across as a loving, devoted couple, but they had things they kept from each other. Or maybe Farthing was fearful of upsetting her.

She came into the house through a side door, then stepped into the sitting-room. She was carrying a small string paper bag with the name of an expensive jewellery store on it. She put her eyes on Priskin, then Sasha. She reached over, took hold of the cat, lifted him off the sofa and put him onto the floor.

"Dimitri has come to collect his car," said Farthing.

"Of course," she said. She was perspiring slightly in the warmth of the house. Her skin was glistening and there was a rosy glow to her cheeks. Her lips were glazed as if she had recently applied a film of lip-gloss to them. Priskin looked at her and she at him.

"How are you Dimitri?" she asked. "I hope you and Olga had a lovely evening," she said. She watched as Sasha took off into the hallway.

"Yes. Very much so. I think I drank a little bit too much of your excellent punch than I should have." She smiled, holding back a chuckle. "I ought to be going and leave you in peace," Priskin said.

She didn't say anything and neither did Dale Farthing. He escorted Priskin towards the front door. As he was about to step out Octavia came into the hallway and lifted her hand as if she had forgotten to mention something. "Pass on my best regards to Olga," she said. "I look forward very much to meeting her again soon," she said.

"She'll enjoy that," said Priskin.

"Russian girls eh," said Farthing. "Friends for life."

"Absolutely," said Priskin. "And thanks for last night. The conversation was great, the food was great and such perfect hosts." He leaned forward, took Octavia gently by the fore-arms and gave her a peck on her cheek. Then he offered his hand to Dale. They shared a solid but brief handshake. None of this namby-pamby palm clenching or fist bumping. It was a man's hand shake.

Farthing opened the door for him and watched him walk to the end of the path, out through the gate and onto the street. Priskin liked the Farthings. They were his kind of people. Sophisticated, wealthy, urbane and friendly. He didn't know how far the friendship would go, whether it would be fleeting like two ships passing in the night or a relationship that would develop into something longer-lasting. What he did know for certain was that Farthing had purchased the Faberge eggs on behalf of his father-in-law. He had learned a lot about the Farthings. That Dale was a kept man. That Octavia kept him as a trophy husband.

Chapter 14

Later that Sunday evening, Priskin received a telephone call from Asamovich. He wanted to see him the following afternoon at three o'clock. This was unusual, because they usually met on a Tuesday afternoon for a review meeting, when Priskin would update him on his finances and keep him abreast of anything significant happening on the financial markets, whether it be a big jump in share price or conversely, a fall.

The next day, Monday, Priskin spent the morning preparing the report he usually gave to Asamovich on Tuesday. When he got to the house in Knightsbridge at three o'clock Asamovich was not resting in the conservatory. He was in a room at the rear of the house that had been converted into a small gymnasium. The room had some loose weights and several exercise machines for a full body workout. He was sitting on an exercise bike. He was wearing a blue tracksuit with a white towel around his neck. He was peddling, non to furiously, on the pedals; still his face was flushed, and the top of his head was peppered with perspiration. His doctor had advised him to lose some weight, through exercise. He had heeded his words. He had taken to cycling a mile, then rowing for the equivalent before picking up the dumb-bells to pump iron for an hour. He had lost maybe half a stone in weight in the last few months. He was taking his doctor's advice seriously. He had also tried to cut out rich foods from his diet. He looked better for it.

He made Priskin wait in the room, standing there watching him on the bike, until the time he set was reached and the alarm on the console rang to tell him to take a rest. Priskin had a document holder in his grip. It contained the report he had prepared.

Out on the garden, the light of day was all but lost to the darkening sky. It had been an okay type of day, weather wise, up until this point. The alarm bell sounded. Asamovich stopped turning the pedals. He gingerly climbed off the bike seat, having a keep a tight hold of the handlebar to stop himself from stumbling. He used the towel to mop the sheen of perspiration off his face. He put his eyes on Priskin.

"I need you to go to Miami," he said.

"When?" Priskin asked.

"In a few days," replied Asamovich.

"Why?" Priskin asked.

"Someone has offered me a five-berth ocean going yacht for twenty million US dollars," Asamovich revealed.

Priskin was surprised. Asamovich had never expressed any desire or interest in buying a yacht.

"Can I afford it?" Asamovich asked.

"I think so," Priskin replied. "Where are you going to keep it?"

"The south of France. With all the others," Asamovich replied.

"Have you considered the overheads?" asked Priskin. "The mooring fees? The upkeep and maintenance of such a vessel?" The conversation was being conducted in Russian.

"Not yet," he replied. "That's why I want you to organise it all. First go to Miami, meet the owner. Take a look at it. Check him out."

"I know nothing about yachts," Priskin admitted.

"I know that. Find someone who does. Take him. Check it out. Give me a report. Make an introduction to the owner on my behalf," Asamovich said.

"Who is the owner?" Priskin asked.

"He's an American called James L. Sinclair. He's a Miami based lawyer," Asamovich said.

Where had this come from? Priskin wondered to himself. It wasn't his usual style. Buying things impulsively, though maybe he had been considering it for some time.

"As you wish," he said. "What's his background?" he asked.

"Who?"

"Sinclair," said Priskin.

"All I know is that he wants to sell a yacht. That's why I want you to go there and look," he replied. He let go of the handlebars and carefully stepped away from the bike. He looked at the document holder in Priskin's hand. "What's in there?" he asked.

"My weekly report," said Priskin.

"Let's go through it tomorrow," Asamovich requested.

"As you wish," said Priskin.

"What about the other matter?" Asamovich said.

"What other matter?" Priskin asked.

"The Faberge eggs," Asamovich snapped.

Priskin decided that honesty was the best policy. "That man I told you about, Dale Farthing, bought them for his father-in-law."

"Who is?" he asked.

"Sergei Molinsky," he replied.

"Gee, I should have known it," said Asamovich, suddenly reverting to English.

"Why should you have known?" Priskin asked.

"He's a collector. But he's never used anyone else to buy things for him."

"The British have slapped an export ban on such items," said Priskin.

"That so," said Asamovich. "How did you discover it was him?" he asked.

"I've met Dale Farthing," said Priskin. "He told me his wife, Octavia, is Molinsky's daughter. It all fits together. Then he told me his father-in-law collects Faberge eggs and other Russian artefacts."

"That's good work," said Asamovich. "Very good work." Priskin said nothing in reply. "Now arrange to go and have a look at the yacht," he said, then he turned to get back on the bike for a second stint.

"I'll need to do some research," said Priskin. "Contact a valuer. Someone who knows what he's talking about were yachts are concerned."

"Do that," said Asamovich in a dismissive way. He took hold of the handlebars, lifted his feet onto the pedals and began to turn them gently, before gradually picking up the pace until the back wheel was spinning at a rapid speed.

Priskin left the house to go home to do some research. He got the impression that Asamovich had forgotten about the Faberge eggs, or perhaps he was testing him and using the yacht as an excuse. He had done a similar thing a year ago when he said he was interested in purchasing an English League Two football club for ten million pounds. He got him to do a lot of investigating, looking at the books of the club and its financial state in terms of assets against liabilities and overheads. It never came to anything. He soon lost interest when he realised that the club had little chance of ever making it into the premier league without spending a huge amount of money on new players. He never had much interest in football. About as much interest as sailing an ocean-going yacht around the Mediterranean. Maybe he was testing him again. Playing a game.

Priskin went home. He got straight onto the task. His priority was to look up James L. Sinclair. Sure enough, there was a Miami based lawyer of that name. He was a genuine lawyer with many rich clients from famous sports people to Florida's old-money establishment figures. He was also seeking to sell his five-berth ocean going boat for close to twenty-eight million US dollars.

Once he had established it all seemed genuine he looked up several companies on the internet who could perform a valuation of a yacht. The request was unusual, in that the vessel was sitting in a dock near to Fort Lauderdale in Florida. Nevertheless, he found the name of a company based in Southampton who specialised in providing valuations and reports of ocean going pleasure craft.

He called the company and spoke to the Managing Director. The company were interested in the assignment. The cost would be five thousand pounds, plus the travel expenses for one of their representatives to fly out to Florida with Priskin to carry out the valuation and to provide a sea-worthiness report. The reports would be ready, one week after the visible inspection had taken place, followed by a sea going trial. Priskin thanked the chap and told him he would get back to him once he had spoken to James Sinclair to arrange a mutual time for the inspections to take place. Once they had the date and a time the company would draw up the terms and conditions of the contract, for him to study and sign. The usual banal stuff.

Chapter 15

On Tuesday afternoon, Priskin went to Knightsbridge for the weekly three o'clock meeting with Asamovich only to discover that he was not at home. Mrs Andropov told him Yuri had left the house this morning with Hector driving the Bentley. His destination was a location on the south coast. When they had chatted yesterday, Asamovich hadn't mentioned anything to Priskin about visiting that part of the country. Priskin left his boss a written note asking him to contact him because he required some additional information about the boat. Such as its tonnage and its sea worthiness certification which the Americans would have issued to the seller. Only then would the company he had contacted about a valuation produce a contract. He still couldn't get his head around why Asamovich wanted to purchase a yacht. He didn't have any sea legs. He would also have to employ people to sail the vessel. Perhaps, he just planned to moor it in St Tropez for the full year or even take it onto the Black Sea where many wealthy Russians had boats.

Two days passed. It was Thursday. Priskin had received an email from Dale Farthing. It was to remind him about the visit to Stamford Bridge on Saturday to watch Chelsea play Burnley in a Premier League fixture. It was also to remind Priskin that he would be meeting his father-in-law, Sergei Molinsky. Priskin was to go to the hospitality unit in the east stand. His name would be on the list of invited guests from the owners of the hospitality boxes at the top of the stand. Several people, including Farthing's friend John

Redmond, the chap who he had met at Farthing's on Saturday night would be attending, plus another one of Farthing's associates. With Sergei Molinsky in attendance it would be a party of five.

Priskin was looking forward to meeting Molinsky, but also watching the game. It was nice of Farthing to invite him. He didn't have to do it. It was only after reading the email that Priskin wondered how Farthing had got his email address. He soon discovered the answer when he spoke to Olga. She was purring with delight. Octavia Farthing had invited her to join her and her close circle of friends for a girls-only Sunday afternoon in a high-end Chelsea bistro. Olga told Dimitri that she had given Octavia both their contact details.

"So that's how Dale Farthing got my email address," Priskin said to her.

"You don't mind. Do you?" Olga asked.

"Not at all," he replied. "No harm done."

"Isn't it great. We have some new friends," she said.

"If it makes you happy. Then it's fine," he said, though he did wonder how long it would last.

Olga didn't respond. She was too preoccupied with making the evening meal to care about what he might have said or thought. His reaction wasn't that important.

At one-thirty, on Saturday afternoon, Priskin left home and made his way to Stamford Bridge, the home of Chelsea Football Club, one of England's top football clubs with a rich history and a list of fans that read like, 'Who's Who'. The late October weather was surprisingly mild. It wasn't woolly hat or gloves chilly today. He was wearing a smart casual padded jacket over a plain open neck shirt and neat slacks.

The crowd, most of whom were wearing replica blue Chelsea home shirts, were milling around the stadium by the time he arrived at five minutes to two. Kick off was in a little over one hour. Therefore, plenty of time to socialise with those in the plush hospitality facilities at the top of the east stand.

The visiting side, Burnley, were not one of the major Premier league teams, so it wasn't a big game. Chelsea were expected to win easily. A ten-pound wager on a home win wouldn't give much of a return. Maybe as little as a pound. Chelsea were at the top of the league, whereas Burnley were near to the bottom of the table.

Priskin was hardly a mad keen football fan, though he didn't have a bad knowledge about English football. This would be the first game he had seen in almost thirteen years. At the age of twenty he had taken a girl from university to a Tottenham Hotspur home game. She was a keen Spurs fan. The after-match squash trying to get out of the ground and the hint of violence and tension in the air between the rival fans, put him off from going again. Thankfully, things had changed in the interim, now the emphasis was on hospitality that, for good or bad, had brought many well-to-do fans into football stadiums.

He made his way through the crowds, into the east stand and into the entrance marked, 'Match Hospitality'. On entering he had to give his name to a uniformed greeter. She gave him a lanyard with his name on it to wear around his neck, then he was directed to an elevator or the flight of stairs to take him to the top of the stand. He took the lift.

The lift doors opened out onto a large banqueting suite in which several dozen people, mostly male, were already assembled. Nearly all of them had a glass of something in their hands. Uniformed waitresses were going through the crowds with glasses of pink champagne on silver trays. On tables placed around the edge of the room were a wide range of foods, both hot and cold dishes. Bottles of wine and soft drinks were placed on a separate table with drinking glasses and whatnot. There was the sound of chit-chat which competed with the sound from the TV screens high on the surrounding walls. There was a combined aroma of curry, fish, and an assortment of other food smells.

The hospitality boxes were across on the pitch side of the banqueting suite. The walls of the room were lined with large glass framed pictures of former Chelsea greats like: Peter Osgood, Charlie Cooke, Bobby Tambling, Peter Bonetti, David Webb and John Hollins.

Priskin could see Dale Farthing, in the centre of the room. He was chatting to someone Priskin didn't know. Farthing turned and clapped his eyes on Priskin coming towards him across the carpeted floor. He excused himself and broke off from the conversation with the other chap.

"Nice of you to make it," he said and held his hand out. Priskin took his hand. "We're in box number ten just along the corridor," said Farthing. "Grab some food. We'll see you in there shortly," he said.

"Sure thing," said Priskin. He made his way across to a table where a waitress was serving hot food from a large hostess trolley. He took a plate, a knife and fork, and joined the line. The talk amongst those standing in the queue wasn't about football, but about business.

When he had a plate of lasagne in his hand he made his away along a corridor to the line of hospitality boxes and soon located the door to number ten. The door was open. John Redmond and another chap were standing in the room chatting. Both had taken a long champagne flute from a table inside the suite which was also lined with bottles of fine wine. On the other side of the room was a freezer full of bottles of beer and cans of soft drinks. An opaque glass sliding door was part of the way open to give a panoramic view of the pitch below. At the other side of the door was an area of two rows of padded seats for those in the box to sit and watch the game. The contrast between the green of the pitch and the blue of the seats in the stands radiated in sharp clarity.

"Hi," said John Redmond to Priskin. "Great to see you. Good of you to join us."

"I wouldn't have missed it for the world," Priskin said. He put the plate of half eaten lasagne on the table. Redmond introduced him to the man he was chatting to. His name was Sam Barnard.

"Take a glass of wine and join us," said Barnard. Priskin did just that, he took a tall, slim glass three quarters full of a fruity wine and put it to his lips. No sooner had he taken the first sip, then a waitress came into the suite to remove the used glasses and plates. The wine, a full-bodied Claret, was very nice.

A roar went up from inside the stadium as the Chelsea players emerged from out of the tunnel to begin their pre-match warm up. This was great, thought Priskin. The view of the pitch was unrestricted, and the hospitality was impressive. Light years away from the last time he had attended a football game. He could live with this standard of food and wine if he had to.

"Been to many games?" Redmond asked him.

"Not many. A few in the past," he replied candidly. He didn't want to say he'd been a regular spectator when he hadn't stepped inside a football stadium in many years.

"Sam was a former director of the club" Redmond said. "He knew Mathew Harding quite well."

Priskin nodded his head, but he had no idea who he was talking about. He looked at Bernard. He was a stout guy, around five ten tall. Saville Row shirt with cuff-links, silk tie, all under a grey made-to-measure suit of the finest quality material. He had a tan that showed off his blue eyes and nice smile. He wore a thin gold band on his wedding finger. His hair was thick and brushed back off a high forehead and matted down with gel. He was holding a glass that contained the bubbly.

The time was getting on for a quarter to three. There was still no sign of Sergei Molinsky. The stadium was now well over three quarters full. The players had left the field after the pre-match warm up. They would be returning shortly to begin the game.

A cry of 'Chelsea, Chelsea' went up from the fans in the north stand, then the club song, 'Blue is the Colour' was played over the public address. Those fans who were wearing blue and claret, the colours of Burnley, where in a section at the opposite side of the ground.

Priskin was just about to step through the open siding door to take a seat outside, when the door to the box opened and a large man in a dark suit appeared. He opened the door, looked inside the room for about three seconds, then he stepped aside. A man who looked to be in his mid-to-late-sixties came into the room, followed by a third man who was as big as the first chap. The second man was Sergei Molinsky. Priskin recognised him from a photograph he had seen on the internet. He was wearing a baggy Saville Row jacket, white shirt, no tie. His dark hair was thinning over a tanned pate. For a man who was in his mid-sixties he looked in good shape. It was obvious that he had had some form of facial surgery.

He put his eyes on Priskin for the first time. One of the other two gentlemen, who must have been his bodyguards, remained standing at the door to the box, whilst the other one accompanied Molinsky to the table. Molinsky took one of the glasses of wine and a napkin off the table.

Dale Farthing stepped forward. "Sergei let me introduce you to a new friend of Octavia's and mine," he said. "Dimitri Priskin from Moscow." Priskin swallowed hard. He switched the wine glass from his right hand into his left hand and held his right hand out. Molinsky took his hand and looked into Priskin's eyes. They shared a brief hand shake. Molinsky had a stiff, sullen look on his face.

"It's a great pleasure to meet you," said Priskin in Russian. Molinsky said nothing. He retained a serious face. Then he stepped forward to the sliding door and looked out onto the pitch. Farthing followed him. "Dimitri works for Yuri Asamovich," said Farthing.

This seemed to get Molinsky's attention in a second. He turned back into the room. "Yuri? How is he?" Molinsky asked Priskin in English. His voice contained a hard Moscow edge to it.

"Very well," he replied.

Molinsky looked towards the two minders in their matching suits and matching bad-ass expressions. Then back at Priskin.

"Извините за безопасность. Мой зять говорит, что я нуждаюсь в них, но я не уверен, что это так," he said, which when translated into English was. '*Sorry for the security. My son-in-law says I need them, but I'm not sure that that's the case.*'

He looked at his son-in-law and gave him a frown. A smile never threatened to crack his face. He was in complete contrast to his daughter who came across as a warm and friendly human being. Her father was someone who liked to play glum and uncompromising. He probably liked the bodyguards being around because they made him feel like someone worth protecting. Priskin detected that Molinsky held his son-in-law in contempt for something. Maybe he didn't like him because he had taken his favourite child from him. Maybe he just didn't like him or trust him. Maybe he was that kind of cold hearted nasty person. A life of business in the rough and tumble of Moscow, in the aftermath of communism, was a good learning ground for those intent on acquiring a good grasp of human character.

"Tell me, where are you from?" he asked Priskin.

"I was born in Moscow."

"When?" asked Molinsky.

"Nineteen eighty-two."

"And your father. What does he do?"

"Did," said Priskin. "He was an official in a Kremlin department under Gorbachev, then Yeltsin. My mother is British. I have dual British-Russian nationality."

"A foot in each camp," said Molinsky. He smiled for the first time then chuckled aloud.

"You could say that," said Priskin smiling.

"I like you," said Molinsky in Russian. "You've got a good sense of humour. You say Yuri is fine? No?"

"Yes. He's fine."

"I last met him one year ago at an event in the Russian embassy." Priskin noticed the word 'last' which seemed to suggest that he knew Asamovich from a previous time. "How many years have you worked for him?" he asked.

"Eight years," Priskin replied.

"Yuri is a fine man. When I met him, I was very impressed with his ability to get things done," Molinsky said. He didn't say which things. Priskin gave him a nod of the head. It was clear that Molinsky knew Asamovich and vice-versa.

Molinsky smiled. He turned his head to say something to his son-in-law, John Redmond, and Sam Barnard.

After some chit-chat had taken place and five minutes had passed the match announcer came over the public address to welcome the two teams onto the pitch. A roar went up from the crowd as the teams emerged from the tunnel and stepped out onto the edge of the field.

Farthing who would have been listening to the conversation went outside onto the step and took a seat next to Redmond and Sam Barnard. Molinsky put the rim of the wine glass to his lips but didn't take a sip.

Down on the pitch the players were going along a line, shaking hands with the opposing side, then the sides split up and took their places in preparation for kick-off. The premier league music played.

"Shall we watch the game together?" Molinsky asked. He gestured to one of the two minders to take the full glass of wine out of his hand. The man came over, took the glass off him, and placed it on the table, mostly untouched.

"Certainly," said Priskin. He accompanied Molinsky out onto the steps and took a seat next to him on the first row. The other three were behind them. One of the minders sat next to Priskin. The other one closed the sliding door but stayed inside the box to guard the door into the room.

The game kicked off in the next minute. Priskin watched from on high. From this distance the players looked like miniature men kicking an orange object about. The blue shirts and shorts of the Chelsea players against the white shirts and sky-blue shorts of the Burnley players were vivid.

Chapter 16

The football game turned out to be a disappointing one-sided affair. Chelsea scored in the first minute when a speculative shot from outside of the penalty box hit a Burnley player on the back-side and cannoned into the goal. The Chelsea fans roared as the ball nestled in the back of the net.

By the end of the first half the score was: Chelsea three - Burnley nil. The game was over as a contest. Molinsky accompanied by his bodyguards paid a visit to the bathroom. The others, including Priskin went into the banquet hall to have a drink. Redmond and Barnard talked about the first half action. Priskin took Dale Farthing to a side.

"Your father-in-law seems like some guy," he said.

Farthing thought about his reply for a long moment. "Depends on what you call some guy," he said through gritted teeth. He poured himself and Priskin a glass of red wine. "He likes to project an image," he said. "Between you and me he's a bit over the top."

Priskin was going to ask him to explain but thought better of it. He let out a chuckle which he was able to stifle in his throat. It came out as little more than a 'huh'. There was some obvious animosity between son-in-law and father-in-law that was reflected in the way they greeted each other. They both had a dislike and mistrust of one another.

Molinsky returned to his seat as the second-half got underway. By sixty minutes the score was four-one to Chelsea. The daylight had long since gone from the sky, but for the merest hint of a wedge of pale blue sky that was lodged beside the edge of a dark cloud. The floodlights were on to illuminate every inch of turf. A fine mist now swirled around the lights on top of the roof of the stand across the pitch. The crowd were not as vociferous as they had been at three o'clock. The result had been decided by half-time. If Burnley made a comeback in this game, it would be like a blind man climbing Everest, unaided.

The final whistle went at just before ten to five. The final score was: Chelsea six - Burnley two. Burnley got a second goal with the last kick of the game which wasn't much more than a consolation.

Molinsky immediately made his farewells. He went around the room and shook hands with Sam Bernard, Redmond, his son-in-law, then Priskin. "It was a pleasure to meet you," he said to him "We should meet some time soon. I'll ask my son-in-law to arrange it."

Priskin noticed that he never called Dale by his name. He was always his son-in-law.

"It will be an honour," replied Priskin.

With that Molinsky was out of there, leaving the scene with his two bodyguards like a VIP at a movie premier. Farthing, Priskin, Redmond and Barnard went into the banqueting room. The catering staff had put out fresh food and drinks so the patrons from the hospitality boxes were back in the room helping themselves to what was on offer.

Priskin, Redmond, and Farthing returned into the box. They stayed there for the next hour to let the crowd drift away before attempting to leave. Priskin and Redmond were chatting when Farthing came over and interrupted to take Priskin to a side. Farthing asked him what his father-in-law had said to him before leaving.

"About meeting with him," Priskin replied.

Farthing looked glum. "He likes you. But don't be fooled by his hospitality. He'll be after something," he warned. His words just about emphasised the sense of mistrust Farthing had for Molinsky. It was a mutual dislike. Priskin thanked Farthing for inviting him to the game. He said goodbye to Redmond, then he took the elevator and left the stadium one and a half hours after the game had ended. He was home, in Notting Hill, for seven o'clock.

On Sunday afternoon, Olga left home for the lunch appointment with Octavia Farthing and her friends in a Chelsea bistro. She was looking forward to an hour of female bonding and chat, followed by lunch and drinks.

Priskin settled down to watch cartoons on TV with Andre at his side. Andre was just about getting over losing 'Purrfect'. He hadn't mentioned the cat for some time.

As soon as Andre lost interest in TV he went to his bedroom to play on his tablet. Priskin went into his study to prepare his weekly report for his boss.

Priskin was typing the report when the telephone rang. He picked up the phone. "Hello," he said. It was Dale Farthing.

"How are you?" Priskin asked him.

Farthing didn't rely. "What are you doing?" he asked. He would have known Olga was out with his wife in the bistro.

"What right now?" Priskin asked.

"Yeah."

"I'm watching TV with my son."

"Is there any chance that we could meet?" Farthing asked.

"What? Now? Right away?" Priskin asked.

"Yeah."

"I'd love to, but I've promised him we'd have some men time."

"Okay," said Farthing. He sounded disappointed.

"Why do you want to meet? What's it about?" Priskin asked.

"I wanted to chat about a proposition," Farthing replied.

"What kind? A business proposition?"

"I don't want to discuss it over the telephone," said Farthing with a mild trace of impatience and conceit in his voice.

"Not a problem. What about tomorrow?" Priskin asked.

"Let's meet tomorrow," said Farthing.

"Where?" Priskin asked.

"Octavia will be at home tomorrow. We'd better make it a neutral location. Your choice."

"I'll be taking my son to school tomorrow morning for nine-thirty," Priskin said. "I can meet you St John's Wood at around ten."

"Where?" Farthing asked.

"There's a coffee house called the, 'The Maiden Over' on St John's Wood by Lord's cricket ground. We can meet in there at ten," Priskin said.

"Fine," said Farthing in a more positive tone of voice. "I'll be there," he confirmed.

"Thanks for yesterday," said Priskin. "It was a great afternoon. I really enjoyed it."

"That's good," said Farthing.

"See you tomorrow."

"Yeah," said Farthing then ended the call.

Priskin turned his mobile phone off. He sank into the comfort of the leather chair. He wondered why Farthing wanted to see him so urgently. It was a bit sudden. It sounded as if he had a proposal to put to him. Priskin was intrigued by this sudden turn of events and what Farthing had to put to him and why it was so important he couldn't discuss it over the telephone. He would find out tomorrow.

Olga returned home a few minutes after five. She said she had had a great time with Octavia and her friends. They had been to a posh eatery in Chelsea called, 'Heaven Sent.' They had discussed a host of things girls do when they get together in a group, like fashion, men, and sex, and all the gossip that was doing the rounds.

She had been invited to meet them again next week at the same time in the same place. She asked Dimitri what he had been doing. He replied that he and Andre had had a quiet afternoon watching cartoons on TV, before Andre had fallen asleep on the sofa. He never mentioned the telephone conversation he had just had with Dale Farthing.

Chapter 17

On Monday morning, it was back to the day job for Priskin. He took Andre to school in his car, arriving there for ten-past-nine. He walked Andre through the gates and into the yard were some boys were kicking a football to each other. He watched Andre join in the game.

He still hadn't received a response from Asamovich about the information he required about the yacht. Maybe he had gone cool on the idea. He could always bring it up with him at the weekly meeting tomorrow, assuming he was home. He may also have gone cool on the Faberge eggs. Maybe he had decided not to pursue them knowing that Sergei Molinsky was the buyer. Molinsky had more money and far more powerful friends than him. There was a rumour that he had several Russian politicians in his back pocket and some friends in the senior ranks of the British government with channels to establishment figures. Priskin had no idea if the rumours were true.

Priskin wondered why Farthing wanted to see him so urgently. He had a mixture of anticipation and apprehension in his thoughts. He recalled Farthing's words about making a business proposal to him. Maybe he wanted to get back at his father-in-law for whom he had little regard. It all sounded a little clandestine. He remembered when he said he didn't wish to discuss the matter on the telephone. Maybe he believed his phone was tapped. It was all a bit cloak and dagger.

The school bell ran at nine-thirty and the kids trooped into the building. Priskin elected to leave his car where he had parked it and walk the short distance to the meeting place which was at the other end of St John's Wood Road.

He walked along Abbey Road, passing Abbey Road Studios, to the junction with Grove End Road, then turned left at the end of the road and onto St John's Road. The tall south stand of Lord's cricket ground was on the other side of the high brick wall. He was dressed casually. Dark sports jacket, jeans, and black trainers on his feet.

The 'Maidan Over' café was in a row of shop outlets at the junction with Wellington Road. The café had a cricket theme with loads of memorabilia, in the form of cricket bats, caps, jumpers, photographs of star players and framed programme covers from famous matches that had taken place down the years at the ancestral home of cricket. The silver topped table and chairs on the pavement outside were currently unoccupied. When there was an important game at Lord's the place would be packed to the rafters.

He stepped under the red canopy, through the door and into the establishment. The words, 'Maidan Over', were stencilled on the plate glass window, in gold letters, on each side of the doorway. He loved the smell of freshly ground coffee beans simmering in a pot and the aroma of freshly baked bagels. It wasn't a greasy spoon. Far from it. There was a 'hissing' sound from a coffee making machine.

Inside a glass counter were a range of chocolate brownies and Danish pastries set out on display.

Dale Farthing was sitting at a table on the right-hand side of the room. He had his head down reading a leaflet or something on the table. The only other customers were a young couple on the other side of the room. A sleeping baby was in the stroller at their side. Music was playing at low volume. The couple were talking in a language that wasn't English.

As Priskin approached the table where Farthing was sitting, the young girl behind the counter came around to greet him. Farthing raised his head and looked at Priskin. He appeared tense and pensive. He had a mug full of coffee in front of him. In the shadow his grey hair looked darker than its natural colour. He looked like a man who made money directing movies or taking photographs. He had that arty-farty creative image about him. He was wearing a fleece jacket zipped up to the neck and dark cord trousers. The shade suited his handsome looks. It was easy to see why such a good-looking man would turn a lady's head. He had a British cool. Maybe that's what Octavia found so attractive.

The waitress took a little book out of an apron pocket and a pen. Priskin asked for a cup of tea, but nothing to eat. He sat down at the other side of the table from Farthing. The baby in the stroller came awake and let out a cry. The attentive father gave his son or daughter a stroke of the cheek.

Farthing looked at Priskin and raised his eyebrows. The baby hadn't quietened down yet. The assistant went behind the counter to make Priskin's beverage.

"How are you?" Priskin asked him.

"Not too bad," Farthing replied, but he seemed distant. Down in the mouth. His shoulders were hunched as if something heavy weighed him down.

Moments passed before the assistant came around the counter, carefully balancing a cup of tea on a saucer. She placed it down on the table in front of Priskin. The tempo of the music playing over the sound-system increased to a foot-tapping pace.

"What can I do for you?" Priskin asked. "Why the secrecy?"

Farthing turned his eyes away from Priskin's face. "I've been thinking about what you told me about Yuri Asamovich," he said.

Priskin pinched his eyes together. "Such has?"

"About him been involved in the killing of that newspaper reporter," he said straight out.

Priskin was put on alert. He had immediate concerns about where this could be heading. He kept his thoughts concealed until he knew what he was driving at.

"I'm not with you," he said.

Farthing took hold of his mug. Priskin glanced behind him at the young couple who were looking into the pram at their baby.

"It's what you told me about the killing. Who knows about it?" Farthing asked. "It's hot," he added.

"What's hot? I don't understand you."

"The information. Someone could make a lot of money from information like that," Farthing said.

Priskin didn't say a word. He lifted the cup of tea from the saucer and put it to his mouth. He took a sip of the liquid. It tasted bitter and lukewarm. He put the cup down into the saucer.

"I'm still not with you Dale. What are you getting at? What's the money connection?" he asked.

"Information about who killed that reporter in Moscow might be worth a lot of money to him."

"To whom?" Priskin asked.

"Asamovich. Of course," replied Farthing.

"He didn't pull the trigger," said Priskin raising his voice a touch. The conversation had instantly turned strange and sinister. The atmosphere between them was suddenly tense.

"Still if he organised it. It must be worth at least ten million to him."

"Ten million. For what?" Priskin asked.

"Not to inform the media. I don't know... the newspapers...
the fucking BBC," said Farthing.

The penny dropped through Priskin's head like a coin
dropping through the cogs of a machine. Farthing was considering
the option of blackmailing Yuri Asamovich over his alleged
involvement in the murder of the journalist.

"Let me get this straight," Priskin said. "You want money
from Asamovich not to inform the newspapers about his *alleged*
involvement in the murder of a newspaper reporter? That's all it is...
alleged," he stressed.

Farthing looked away from him. Priskin continued. "There's
no evidence. Without evidence its worthless. It's like. I don't
know..." he paused to think of a suitable example. "It's like
accusing the Israelis of killing Robert Maxwell, then throwing him
off his yacht. There's no evidence. Don't you think the Russian
justice system would have pursued him if they had evidence of his
involvement?" he said.

Farthing considered his words for a few brief moments.
"He'll give me ten million pounds to stop me from going to the
newspapers. I've done some research. He was questioned by the
Moscow police and..."

Priskin interrupted him in mid-sentence. "Him and about two
dozen others," he said. "Dale. Please forget about it." He stopped
short of calling him an idiot, but then changed tact. "You've really

got to be joking. There's no evidence to link him with it. Those who organised it covered their tracks. Got someone else to do it. It's like the Kennedy killing. It was all covered over. It's all hearsay. Don't you think the Moscow police looked into it? Of course, they did," he said, answering his own question.

Farthing suddenly didn't appear to be as cocksure as he had two minutes ago. There was a look in his eyes that suggested he was reconsidering the idea. Was he so desperate for money that he had come up with this ludicrous plan?

"Are you seriously considering trying to blackmail Yuri Asamovich?" Priskin asked.

"Yeah. And I want you to help me do it."

"How?" Priskin asked.

"By recording him admitting it," Farthing said.

Priskin pulled back in his seat. "That's crazy," he said in such a strong voice that the couple looked over in his direction. He looked at them fleetingly, then swiftly averted his eyes from theirs.

"You're dealing with a serious player," said Priskin, reducing the volume of his voice to little more than a whisper. "He won't roll over in a million years. If I put a red-hot blow-torch to his balls and told him to admit it. He still wouldn't. He knows people back in Moscow who will deal with you and me and leave us for dead. No matter if you're father-in-law is Sergei Molinsky or not. He wouldn't give you a hundred pounds never mind ten million." He refrained from calling Farthing something he might regret.

He paused as the young couple began to collect their belongings together. They asked the counter assistant for the bill. Just then the bell at the door jingled and two burly men in dusty work gear entered the café. They began a loud conversation about what they wanted to drink.

Priskin looked at Farthing. "Dale, you need to forget about this. It's not going to work or go anywhere," he said.

Farthing bit his lower lip. He hadn't only not thought it through in a logical manner, but he hadn't considered what Priskin's reaction would be. It was an impulsive idea that he hadn't fully considered and taken all the implications into account.

"Let's forget we ever had this conversation," said Priskin almost pleading. "I don't want our friendship to end on the strength of this for the sake of our wives. You've got to forget about it," he said.

Farthing didn't reply. Though he did look taken aback and a little shaken by Priskin's words. The door to the café opened for a second time in quick succession and two more workmen entered. Priskin decided this was a good time to get out of the cafe. He put the cup into the saucer.

"I'll be seeing you," he said. He got up from the table, leaving his hardly touched beverage on the table, walked to the door and out of the café. He didn't look back at Farthing.

Chapter 18

On leaving the café Priskin walked back along St John's Wood Road. He just couldn't get over what Farthing had proposed to him. That he use a recording device to tape Asamovich admitting that he had organised the murder of the newspaper journalist. It was almost too incredible for words. Farthing had suddenly changed beyond all recognition. He was no longer the easy going, mild mannered man. Now he came across as a desperate paranoid schizophrenic who was hell bent on taking them both down.

Priskin hoped he was wrong, but their friendship was tottering on the edge of a deep precipice. As he walked onward he went over the conversation several times. He concluded that he could have been right all along. Octavia had all the money. Maybe the marriage wasn't everything it was cracked up to be and that's why Farthing sought to try and blackmail Asamovich. He must have been desperate for money to come up with such an absurd plan. The daftest part of it was his assumption that he would help him blackmail his boss. Farthing didn't know Asamovich as well as he did.

As soon as Priskin got into his car he started the engine and set off. He drove home to Notting Hill, arriving home for eleven o'clock. Olga had just come in from spending some time at a local supermarket buying several items they had missed from the weekly shop. He never mentioned anything about meeting Farthing. He knew how close she was becoming to Octavia and her friends. That could complicate matters. He went into his study, closed the door, and began to work on the weekly report for his boss.

He had just completed the report when his mobile phone rang. He instantly recognised the number it was Dale Farthing. He accepted the call.

"Hello," he said.

"Sorry," said Farthing. "I was out of order," he admitted.

Priskin felt a little anguish. He didn't know whether to tell him not to call him again, not now or ever, but his humanistic side came to the front. "All right," he said. "Let's forget about the conversation. Assume it never happened," he said.

"Can we still be friends?" Farthing asked.

"Of course," Priskin replied. "This won't affect me as long as we never discuss it again."

"Of course," said Farthing. "Never again."

"In that case we'll forget about it."

"Good," said Farthing. "Thanks for been so understanding."

"I'll speak to you later…and thanks for calling," Priskin said.

Farthing said nothing else. He terminated the call. Priskin blew out a sigh of relief. He felt better already. He smiled to himself. He was pleased that Farthing had had the courage to call him to apologise and seek to pave the way to an understanding. Hopefully, he had seen sense and would never ever mention it again. Priskin felt a sense of satisfaction, but also one of impending gloom at the same time. Olga was becoming close to Octavia. If Farthing did come up with a crazy scheme to get money out of Asamovich, Asamovich would put two and two together. He would know that Priskin had given the blackmailer the information. He wasn't stupid.

He rewrote the report for Asamovich, then at around three in the afternoon he returned to St. John's Wood to collect Andre from school. Andre had had a good day. He told his daddy that he was going to be in the school's Christmas nativity play. He was playing one of the three wise men. He handed his father a letter from the school detailing the items he required, like a bathrobe and a gold paper covered box to make his gold gift to the baby Jesus look authentic. Priskin had to smile to himself.

After the evening meal he turned his PC on to check for any emails. An email from Asamovich was waiting in the in-box. As he expected he had gone off the idea of purchasing the yacht. All the plans were put on hold, which meant they would never see the light of day again. It was nothing unusual. Was Asamovich testing him? Keeping him on his toes. Priskin emailed him back to acknowledge the message, then he sent an email to the company in Southampton to thank them for their advice. It was now unlikely that he would be planning to travel to Fort Lauderdale to view the yacht. His third and final email was to the travel agent he had spoken to about airline tickets to Miami. He apologised to them and thanked them for the quotes they had sent him, but he wouldn't be needing them now.

After sending the messages he turned the PC off, went into the lounge and poured himself a vodka, then he returned to his study. He wondered what his plan of action would be if Farthing decided to pursue his stupid scheme to attempt to blackmail Asamovich. He had several options open to him. He could try and silence Farthing for all time by hiring a hitman to kill him. That would be too dodgy. He would soon become a suspect, after all he had recently become a friend of his. That would shine a light on him. The police would question the likes of John Redmond and Sam Barnard. They would mention Farthing's friendship with Priskin. That would put him in the frame.

He could agree to assist Farthing blackmail Asamovich. If he covered his back, he might get away with it. He could even consider telling Asamovich what Farthing was planning to do and admit that he had given him information. Asamovich would then be put in a dilemma about what to do with Farthing. Maybe that wouldn't be such a good idea. His third option was to contact Sergei Molinsky and inform him what his son-in-law was up to in the hope that he would tell him to drop it. The final option was to do nothing. Farthing might have already concluded that it was a non-starter. There was no evidence to link Asamovich to the murder of the journalist. After considering his options he decided to do nothing in the hope that Farthing had seen sense.

The following day, Tuesday, Priskin took a cab from Notting Hill to Knightsbridge to pay Asamovich a visit for their weekly meeting. When he arrived at the house, Hector, his valet, and chauffeur was washing the Bentley.

Asamovich was in a light-hearted mood. Something had taken his fancy, but he didn't tell Priskin what it was. He informed Priskin that he had gone off the idea of buying the yacht because the seller, James L. Sinclair, the big-league, Miami lawyer, had been summoned to appear before a judge in a Miami federal courthouse on a tax evasion charge. This would only make a potential purchase of the yacht more complicated, so he had gone off the idea. Priskin said it was a wise decision. Not quite, said Asamovich. The plan was on the back-burner, simmering under a low light. The outcome of the hearing would determine if he went back into the market for the boat. If there was a chance that Sinclair would be fined, then he might offer him less than the twenty-eight million asking price. Especially if he needed capital quickly to pay a fine. Other than the purchase of the yacht, Yuri didn't say a lot, but he did show Priskin a sales brochure of a property on the south coast, near to Brighton, that he was interested in buying.

He wanted Priskin to go to the south coast the following day to look at the house to see what his initial opinion was. It was a six-bedroomed property overlooking the English Channel with views across to the rolling Sussex Downs in the distance. It would be his castle in the English countryside.

Priskin had little experience of looking at property and assessing its value. He told Asamovich, but he still said he wanted him to go there to take a look and to give him a report. Asamovich gave him the sales brochure and asked him to make an appointment with the agent selling the property on behalf of the vendor. The asking price was seven and a half million pounds.

Chapter 19

The following day, Wednesday, Priskin drove to the south coast. The property Asamovich wanted him to look at was situated near to the town of Rottingdean. The location was not far from the eastern edge of the Brighton area where it met the Sussex Downs. It was a nice property, situated on a winding hilly road on a wide plateau between two hillsides. It was a twenty-first century futuristic design over two floors. Twenty acres of land were set on each side of the house. There was more than enough space to erect a large garage to house Asamovich's vintage car collection. From the front elevation the upper rooms had a panoramic view of the English Channel. In the spring and summer months it would be a delightful spot. In autumn and winter, maybe not such a nice place. A six-foot-high brick wall surrounded the property on all four sides. There was a ditch at the rear to catch the rainwater coming down the hillside

Priskin met the estate agent, a pompous little man in a pinstriped suit. The chap showed him around the property. The glass enclosed swimming pool and the gym at the rear of the house were certainly two of the key selling points along with the views and the ultra-modern design. The main living area had an open plan lounge and open plan kitchen and dining room combination with a dividing glass wall and sloping glass roof. The privacy was provided by a screen of tall trees at the rear. It didn't require much in the way of redecoration or work as all twenty rooms were well decorated and maintained. A combination of wind and solar power supplied the power. It was in such contrast to the Knightsbridge mansion. Priskin thought seven and a half million pounds was a fair asking price. The land provided privacy and the potential to build other living quarters or even a stable. Horses could graze in the field. He did wonder if this was another one of Asamovich's games, but maybe he was serious about having a second home or even moving out of London, full stop. Of course, this had implications for Priskin and his family. If his boss did move out of London would this mean he would have to relocate nearer to him? There was no reason he should, but maybe it wouldn't be such a bad idea.

He spent the afternoon looking around the house, then drove along the coast road and into Brighton. Looking at the house and around to area certainly took his mind off Dale Farthing for a few hours. It had now been over two days since he had heard from him. It was three weeks since he and Larry Mitchie had broken into Farthing's house. It was almost becoming a peripheral memory to the events that had subsequently happened.

He drove back to London, arriving home in Notting Hill at seven o'clock in the evening. He got straight onto his computer and typed up his thoughts and observations on the house.

Early the next morning, Priskin emailed Asamovich with his summary about the property in a two-thousand-word report. He highlighted the potential value of the land, the solidness of the structure, but also recommended that a full surveyors report be sought before going into any negotiation about the price with the vendor. He said he thought the asking price was fair, though an offer of seven million in cash might persuade the vendor as the agent said the seller was keen on a quick sale.

At a time, close to one o'clock in the afternoon Priskin's smart phone rang. He recognised the number in the window. It was Dale Farthing calling. It was with a combined sense of apprehension and eager anticipation that he answered the phone. It was over three days since they had met in, 'The Maidan Over'.

"Hello Dale," he said.

"Hi Dimitri. How are you?" Farthing asked in a cheery tone of voice.

"Fine," he replied. In the back of his mind he asked himself what he wanted. "What can I do for you?" Priskin asked.

"My father-in-law called me last night. He said he wants to meet you. Said how much he was impressed by you."

"Okay," said Priskin. He had gotten the impression that Molinsky would want to speak to him to ask him how Asamovich was. He seemed like the kind of person who wanted to be kept up-to-date on how other rich Russians were doing. Maybe he would ask him to become an informant.

"Where? And at what time?" he asked.

"He'll be at the Park Lane Hilton in Mayfair tomorrow night attending a charity function. Can you make it for the pre-drinks at eight o'clock? He has a suite on the third floor. He won't be expecting you to stay for the event or anything like that."

"Will you be there?" Priskin asked.

"No. I won't be there. I'm accompanying Octavia to an event near to our home. Why?"

"Just asking," he said. "Please tell your father-in-law that I will be delighted to meet with him," Priskin said.

"I'll inform him," Farthing said. He rang off after saying goodbye. It was as if Monday had never happened. Priskin was instantly suspicious but didn't know why. Maybe he was being a little too cautious. Maybe Farthing had told Molinsky about the connection between Asamovich and the murder of the newspaper journalist. But he would already know this. Still it sounded like an opportunity to meet with Molinsky. One of the big-hitters in London's Russian community. The meeting might be nothing more than a quick hello and a handshake.

Asamovich emailed Priskin to thank him for his in-depth report and the recommendations there in. It seemed as if he was keen to press ahead with the purchase of the house. He instructed Priskin to employ a surveyor to carry out a full survey of the property, but also to instruct a surveyor to calculate the value of the land and the potential to add a building to house his collection of thirty vintage cars. The cars would be close to him instead of being in a building half way across London. The final paragraph of the email seemed to suggest that he was seriously considering relocating to the south coast. He asked Priskin to begin looking for an agency to market his Knightsbridge home. He wanted a minimum of fifty million pounds. Over three times as much as he had paid for it. Six times the cost of the property on the south coast. It appeared that he was cashing in on the spiralling cost of London property.

Priskin began the tasks immediately. First, he looked for a surveyor to carry out the survey on the Sussex property. His second task was to find a London based property agent who could undertake the task of putting the Knightsbridge property on the market.

Chapter 20

On Friday night, Priskin donned his best suit, a fresh shirt with a silk tie. He set off to Mayfair in a black cab. The cabbie dropped him off under the semi-circular canopy outside of the hotel. The time was ten minutes to eight. He liked to be punctual more than anything in the world. He disliked people who missed appointments because of their poor time keeping.

The fifteen floors of the hotel soared into the night sky. Traffic was zooming along Park Lane. Across the road was the dark, tree-lined expanse of Hyde Park. The streets of Mayfair were on this side of the thoroughfare. The building housing the hotel must have been more than fifty years old, but it was still one of London's foremost locations for events for its position in the heart of the city was prime real estate.

Priskin stepped into the marble coated foyer, then sauntered across to the information desk. There was a sign on a podium which said: 'Welcome to the 'Guild of British Charity Organisations'. Beyond, through a set of glass doors was the ballroom in which it was possible to see a score or more tables that had been set-out in a cabaret formation.

A pretty girl in a jacket and a matching waistcoat and blouse was standing at the counter. She greeted him with a warm smile.

"Mr Molinsky's suite please," he said.

She looked at him through wide sparkling eyes. "Is he expecting you?" she enquired.

"Yes."

"Your name please?"

"Dimitri Priskin."

People in evening wear were stepping into the ballroom, from where violin music was playing, and the smell of spicy food was escaping. She consulted the screen on the monitor before her, tapped in a few commands and looked at the resulting information. She lifted her eyes to him and smiled.

"Mr Molinsky is expecting you. Suite ten. On the third floor," she said. "You may use the elevator," she pointed to the lift door on the other side of the foyer. "Turn to your right out of the elevator on the third floor. Suite ten is along the corridor on the same side. I'll inform your party that you are on your way," she said.

He thanked her, then set off across the foyer. Party goers and guests to the event were congregating in an area adjacent to the ballroom. Staff in uniform were coming and going from the kitchen area, carrying silver trays, and wheeling hostess trolleys through the doors.

He called the elevator. A car was soon at the ground floor. He stepped in, looked at himself in the mirror and took the opportunity to adjust the knot of his tie and pat down his hair. Here was his opportunity to impress Molinsky further with his style and charm.

Molinsky was a busy man. He wouldn't have invited him here just to say 'hello'. He had invited him here for a reason. Just what that reason was he wasn't sure. It had been a little under a week since he had met him at the football game, therefore the invitation to meet him so swiftly after that was a sign that he had something to put to him.

When the elevator reached the third floor, he stepped out, turned to the right and went along a wide carpeted corridor that was semi-circular in shape. Antique Queen Anne tables holding gold plated bowls containing flowers lined the corridor. Picture frames that displayed famous London landmarks were attached to the wall at equal lengths.

He came to the door of suite ten, waited for a moment to straighten his jacket, then knocked at the door. The time was two minutes to eight.

The door was opened by a man in a dark suit. Priskin recognised him as one of the bodyguards he had seen at Stamford Bridge last Saturday. He was a large thick-set guy with a military posture and a menacing presence. His hair was thick on top, chopped short down the sides. He looked Priskin up and down for a few seconds before stepping to a side, opening the door wide and inviting him into the suite with a wave of his hand. He didn't say a word.

Priskin stepped into an enclosed room which was illuminated by a crystal chandelier hanging from the ceiling. The walls were a shade of gold and engraved in silver braiding. A second man who resembled the first man was standing close to a double-door that led into the suite. The decoration was A1, the carpet a deep rich assortment of blues, reds, and greens in a twisting pattern.

The second man opened the double doors. Priskin wondered if he was going to be frisked. He wasn't. He was shown into a lounge room. Sergei Molinsky was sitting on a wide white sofa, against a side wall with his legs stretched and resting on a foot stool. He had a large, thick cigar in one hand and a glass of bubbly in the other. He was dressed in evening wear, so he had somewhere to go later. Out of open curtains at a balcony door was a view across the dark terrain of Hyde Park, but for the glow of lampposts on the footpaths cutting across the grassland.

Molinsky clapped his eyes on Priskin and gave him a smile. He held his hand out for Priskin to take. They exchanged a firm handshake. "Very nice of you to come and see me," said Molinsky. "I won't keep you long," he said in Russian.

"It's very nice of you to invite me," replied Priskin in Russian.

A door in the side opposite the sofa came upon and a man who wasn't Dale Farthing entered the suite. He was someone Priskin had never seen before. He looked to be Molinsky's age, but didn't have the expensive clothes or the look of great wealth. He was wearing a grey suit, pink tie, dark shirt. He looked gaunt and had an olive tint to his flesh.

"Dimitri, I'd like you to meet my good friend Leonid Chavan. Leonid is my assistant. He looks after me well," he said in English. Leonid looked in Priskin's direction and nodded his head, sagely. "Take a seat," Molinsky said to Priskin. He did as requested and plumped down into the softness of a stout armchair. Molinsky held the burning end of the cigar a distance from his face, then he placed the champagne flute on a table at the side of the sofa.

"You must be wondering why I have invited you here?" he said. Priskin nodded his head but refrained from saying anything until he was asked a question that required a direct response. Molinsky continued. "I have heard good things about you from my son-in-law," he said.

"That's very kind of him," said Priskin.

"Why don't you come and work for me?" Molinsky said. "Leonid is returning home to retire to his dacha by the Black Sea." Chavan remained impassive and standing by the sofa.

"A job?" Priskin asked.

"How much does Asamovich pay you?" Molinsky asked.

"Well…"

"No. Don't tell me. That is, how the British say… Too intrusive," Molinsky admitted. "I will give you double what he pays you," he said.

Priskin retained a level disposition. "That's very generous. Thank you," he said.

"You will consider my offer?" Molinsky asked.

"I will be honoured to consider your offer," said Priskin. "What's the job?" he asked.

"You'll do everything you do for Asamovich. Take control of my finances. Manage my portfolio of properties. Be my escort to business meetings. Arrange my travel. Book hotel rooms. That kind of thing," he said. He paused for a moment to put the cigar to his lips and take in a cloud of fumes, then let it out through his mouth. "You'll even buy my cigars," he added.

"It's a very generous offer," said Priskin.

"You'll consider it then?"

"Yes. Definitely."

"Yuri is a good man. He will find someone else to look after him." Priskin gave him a smile but said nothing. "You will let me know in a few days?" Molinsky asked.

"I will," said Priskin. It immediately crossed his mind, that Farthing had set him up for this. That is suggestion that they blackmail Asamovich was nothing more than a test of his loyalty. As he hadn't caved in and abandoned Asamovich he had passed the test.

The side door opened. A gorgeous looking lady who was wearing a sparkling black gown entered the room. She was around forty-years-of-age and had a trim figure. She had shoulder length blonde hair in a stylish, flowing cut. She was carrying a small clasp type of handbag in her hands.

Molinsky got up from off the sofa. Priskin followed his lead and got to his feet.

"Please consider my offer," said Molinsky. "I will be holding a dinner party at my apartment next week. I'd like to invite you and your wife to attend. Leonid will give you the details," he said. "Perhaps you can give me your decision at that time."

"I will be pleased to do that," said Priskin. Molinsky held his hand out. Priskin took his hand for a second handshake. Molinsky escorted the lady to the door leading into the ante-room and stepped out with her, arm-in-arm.

Chavan took Priskin to a side. He withdrew a business card from a jacket pocket and handed it to Priskin. "Here is my card," he said in Russian. "Give me a call in a day or two. I'll give you the details of the dinner party," he said.

"When is it?" Priskin asked.

"Tuesday the tenth."

"Where?"

"At Mr Molinsky's apartment overlooking the Thames."

"What time?" Priskin asked.

"I'll let you know," he replied.

"Thank you," said Priskin looking at the contact details on his card.

Chavan led Priskin to the exit, then through the door and out onto the corridor. He escorted him to the elevator and made sure he was on his way down to the ground floor. He didn't say another word.

Priskin slipped the card into his packet pocket. He ran a fingertip along the sharp edge. He was delighted to receive the job offer, but still a little cautious, though, it did seem genuine. Leonid Chavan looked to be retiring age. He was probably going home to retire by the Black Sea.

Instead of returning home immediately, Priskin visited a wine bar on the Piccadilly side of Mayfair and sat at the bar with a glass of Chianti. He wondered if the proposal from Farthing was little more than a test to check his loyalty. He had no way of knowing.

Chapter 21

On Saturday morning, the Priskin family went to a local supermarket to do the weekly shop. Dimitri didn't mention to Olga about the job offer from Molinsky, nor did he tell her about Asamovich expressing a wish to move out of London to the south coast and the plan to sell his Knightsbridge home.

The remainder of Saturday was quiet. Priskin spent the afternoon with Andre playing touch rugby in the back garden. With the change of the clocks at the back-end of October the evening was getting dark at four-thirty. They were back inside for something to eat at a quarter to five. Andre loved spaghetti-on-toast. The more Priskin thought about the job with Molinsky then the more he thought about his son. Living in London was becoming a bit of a struggle. There was too much crime, too much wondering if some nut-job would set off a bomb on an underground train. Too many sad stories. It was time to get out of London. He knew that Olga was becoming anxious about the quality of life in the capital.

In the early evening the family settled down to watch TV. After Andre had gone to bed at nine, Priskin went into his study to do some homework on estate agents. There were any number of agents who sold high-end properties who would be keen to put the mansion on the market, not just to clients in the UK, but throughout the Middle East, Japan, and North America.

On Sunday morning, Olga had just served a light late breakfast when Priskin's phone rang. It was Dale Farthing. Despite reservations Priskin went into his study to take the call. Farthing wanted to know how the meeting with his father-in-law had gone and what he wanted to speak to him about.

"Don't you know?" Priskin asked.

Farthing said he didn't, which Priskin found surprising. "Perhaps you ought to ask him," he said replying to his initial question. "Our conversation will remain private," he added.

The rebuff seemed to upset Farthing. "I've got another plan," he blurted out.

"About what?" Priskin asked.

"Not over the telephone," said Farthing.

Priskin felt his heart drop and his anger rise. "You're still not thinking about that plan to blackmail Asamovich are you?" he asked. "I thought we agreed that you would drop it before it got out of control."

"I've had a rethink," said Farthing.

"I told you there's no evidence. It's all rumour. There's nothing to it."

"No. Another plan," Farthing said in an ominously sounding tone of voice. "Meet me tomorrow in that cafe. I'll put it to you.

Same time tomorrow." He didn't wait for Priskin to say okay. He ended the call without uttering another word.

Once again Priskin questioned Farthing's sanity. He hadn't given up the idea or perhaps he had concocted another crazy plan to get money out of Asamovich. Where this might end Priskin had no idea.

Olga left the house at one o'clock to meet with Octavia and her friends for the luncheon appointment. Priskin was pleased that she was getting out and meeting new people who shared the same interests as her. She was in her element.

Later that afternoon he received an email from Asamovich. Once again, he thanked him for the report in regard to the house in Sussex. He said he had made up his mind. He was selling-up in London to move to Sussex to live in a place free from the noise, the pollution and the congestion of the city. Priskin replied that he had sent an email to several London estate agents who dealt in properties well over the average asking price. He would let him know of progress when he met him on Tuesday. Asamovich said 'okay'.

Monday morning dawned cold and grey. It was 'Guy Fawkes' day on Thursday. Andre had asked for some fireworks. He told his mother that the parents of his friends at school had bought them some. On the strength of that his mum said they would get him a small number of fireworks. He could have a few of his school friends to the house for hot-dogs and soup, whilst the grown-ups supervised the fireworks. It was a purely British celebration, but they wouldn't deny him the joy of watching fireworks going off.

After she put it to him, Dimitri told Olga he would purchase a box of sparklers and fireworks from a local store on his return from taking Andre to school. He took his son to school, parked just around the corner and walked Andre into the yard. He waited until the bell rang at nine-thirty and Andre had entered the building before he left and walked through St John's Wood to the, 'Maiden Over' café at the junction of St John's Road and Wellington Road.

Farthing was already inside. He was sitting at the same table they had occupied this time last week. The smells and the sounds were the same. A man and a woman were sitting at a table in the corner. On an overcast day like today the cricket memorabilia didn't seem quite as fascinating as it would on a warm summer day.

Farthing had a mug of coffee in front of him, plus a half-eaten chocolate biscuit. Priskin didn't know how he was going to play this, perhaps it was time to stop pulling his punches. Perhaps it was time to put it too him straight. If he carried on with this bullshit it would end very badly for him. First, he had to hear what Farthing had to say.

Similar music to that of last Monday was playing over the airwaves. The same member of staff as last week was in attendance. In her starched uniform she looked very pretty.

Priskin sat at the table. He asked for a bottle of sparkling water and a glass. He was tempted by the sight of a cream cake slice but decided against it. He was watching his weight. He sat across the table from Farthing who looked sullen and glum. How had their friendship turned so bad? So quickly? The man was becoming a weight he couldn't jettison or a bad cold he couldn't shake off.

Farthing was wearing a fleece. His grey hair revealed a tint of silver root.

"What is it this time?" Priskin asked.

Farthing remained stony faced and prickly. He glanced at the two people at the other side of the room. A splash of rain began to drop onto the road outside at the same time as a red London bus went by the window.

"I want a million pounds," he said.

"Last week it was ten million," said Priskin. "Are you aiming lower?"

"A million is more realistic."

"Is this some kind of a sick joke?" Priskin asked. "I told you Asamovich can't be touched. There's no evidence."

"I didn't say anything about Asamovich," said Farthing.

"Who then?" Priskin asked. Before Farthing could answer the waitress placed a bottle of water and a glass on the table in front of Priskin. He thanked her, watched her move away then he pulled the cap off the bottle.

"You," said Farthing.

Priskin was stunned. "Me?" he said in startled amazement. "You want a million pounds from me. You really have gone mad." Farthing retained his mute expression. "Why do you think you'll get a million pounds from me?" Priskin asked.

"For not telling Asamovich what you told me."

Priskin wanted to act unconcerned, put on an aloof front and seem blasé to his words. He put the bottle to his lips and took in a quarter of the content. The bubbles went up his nose which caused him to sneeze. He rubbed the base of his nostrils with a fore finger.

"Excuse me," he said. Farthing said nothing. "If I had a million pounds. Which I don't. Why would I give it to you?" He felt the urge to lunge out and punch Farthing in the face, but it wouldn't look good in here. There were too many witnesses to see it.

"He'll be most unhappy that you told me his secrets," said Farthing.

"What secrets?" Priskin asked.

"About his past. Embezzling millions of dollars from an EU fund designed to help Russia's development after the collapse of communism. Using it to buy companies to float shares on the stock market to make lots of money. His art collection. The Van Gogh, the Paul Gaugin. The vintage cars."

"Its common knowledge," said Priskin. "He's got nothing to hide," he added.

"Yeah, but the way he got his money. That's a different story."

"I beg to differ. Everyone was at it in Russia. The place was a thief's paradise. An Aladdin's cave. You'll have to do better than this," said Priskin. He forced a grim expression onto his face. A game of cat and mouse had developed. A game of chess, but without the board or the pieces.

"I have to commend you," said Farthing.

"On what?" Priskin asked.

"Your use of metaphors. It's really impressive."

"I learned the use of language from an early age. Listening to my mother when she would tell me off."

"You're getting off the subject," said Farthing.

"Which is?" Priskin asked.

"I want a million pounds. Either that or you get me one of his paintings to sell or you sell it on the black market. That, or I'll make an appointment to see Yuri and tell him what you told me."

"Have you ever tried to sell stolen works of art on the black market?" Priskin asked. He put the bottle to his lips and took in a mouthful of water.

Farthing didn't answer the question. "Have you?" Priskin asked. Just then the door to the café opened and three people entered. A middle-aged couple and an elderly lady. They sat at the table next to Priskin and Farthing. Meanwhile the music changed. Fleetwood Mac sang about a 'Gypsy'.

"It's still a million either way," said Farthing.

"You don't have the balls," said Priskin.

"Try me." The middle-aged couple overheard Farthing's words and looked at Priskin. Priskin edged closer to the table.

"Look. I haven't got that kind of money," he said in a semi whisper.

"I think you have," said Farthing.

"Why?" Priskin asked.

"Asamovich must pay you well and I bet you've been dealing from the top of the deck. I bet you've amassed quite a fortune by now," Farthing said.

"Believe me, I've nowhere near that. Anyway, why are you so desperate for money? Why don't you ask your father-in-law for it?" he asked.

"He hates me," Farthing replied.

"Why? What have you done that's so bad that he doesn't like you?" he asked. Farthing didn't reply. Priskin continued. "He's your wife's father for crying out loud."

He was seeking to get him off the idea of asking him for money. He felt a little sorry for him. Was he fearful that his marriage would end, and he'd be left without a penny to his name?

"I still want a million from you," said Farthing. "I'll give you one week to get it," he said with a determined tone in his voice. "And, there's something else I know about you," he added.

"What?"

"I know that you stole the cat."

Priskin looked at him but didn't reply. The look on his face must have been a giveaway. Farthing saw it. He beamed a half-smile. "I knew it from the moment I saw your reaction when Octavia told you how much he's worth. His true value. I saw it on your face."

Priskin was stunned into silence. Farthing took a sip of the coffee. Then put the mug down. He continued. "Then when I knew you worked for Asamovich I worked it out." He still maintained the smirk on his face, like a dog who had found a juicy bone.

Priskin changed his posture. The hard edge of the chair was grating into the back of his legs. "Okay," he mouthed.

"I wondered why anyone would want to break into my house but take nothing other than Sasha. You were looking for the eggs. Probably on Asamovich's order. Is that right?"

Priskin concluded that seeking to deny it was futile. He soulfully nodded his head.

"I thought so. If I don't get the money. I'll tell Octavia that it was you. She'll quickly end her friendship with Olga."

Priskin looked into his eyes. "Leave the ladies out of it," he warned.

Farthing looked smug and full of self-congratulation. He made a 'huh' sound, as if he was mocking Priskin. "You must think I'm stupid," he said.

Priskin had to admit to himself that Farthing had him over a barrel. "A week eh?" he asked. "Doesn't give me a lot of time to get it," he added. He was aware that the couple on the next table were conscious of the animosity between the two men on the table near to them. Their body language was telling a story of its own. He didn't want it to get out of hand.

"I'll have to think about it," he said. "If I can help you I will." He had changed tack to try and appease Farthing.

"No good," said Farthing. "I don't think Asamovich will be happy when I tell him you've been talking about him behind his back."

Priskin didn't have an answer to that. He was guilty has charged. "Okay," he said. "Leave it with me for a week. I'll try to help you," he added.

Farthing appeared to be upset by the suggestion that he needed help. "There's no help required," he said in a piqued tone.

"So why do you want a million?" Priskin asked.

"Long story," he replied in a more thoughtful, introspective tone of voice.

Priskin didn't reply. He had to stay in check of his emotions which were eighty percent in favour of smacking him in the mouth. Farthing was a big man, but he wasn't big man tough. Priskin pulled his chair back and got to his feet. "Leave it with me," he said. "I've got to go. I've got other things to do."

"Contact me in a week," said Farthing. "Let me know what you're going to do."

Priskin nodded his head in his direction. He backed away from the table and stepped out of the café, taking the remainder of the water in the bottle with him. On stepping out into the weak watery sunlight he lifted the collar of his jacket to his neck, though it provided little protection against the icy northerly blast of air.

He had to consider his options all over again. What did he do with Farthing? Did he give him a million pounds? Did he steal one of Asamovich's paintings and give it to him? Did he tell

Asamovich? Did he do nothing in the hope that Farthing would drop it and never ever raise the subject again? Or did he kill Farthing? The final option was the one that would give him the most satisfaction, but it was far too problematic. There was a final option. That was to seek a meeting with his father-in-law to inform him what his son-in-law had in mind. Molinsky might be able to persuade him to drop it. The seven days Farthing had given him to think about it had given him some breathing space. But he would like to sort it out sooner rather than later.

Chapter 22

On arriving home, Priskin concentrated on other matters. Such as the house move Asamovich was mooting. He contacted an estate agent called, 'Heath and Horner', who dealt in high-end house marketing. He asked them to act on behalf of Asamovich. They agreed a one-off flat fee to market the mansion. Then he wrote an email to the agent acting for the vendor of the house in Sussex and offered them an opening bid of seven million pounds for the house and the twenty acres of land, as per Asamovich's instruction. All the time he was thinking about what to do with Farthing. He now had his work cut out to balance the sale and purchase of the houses as well as dealing with Farthing. The more he thought about him, the more he wanted to kill him. He knew he wouldn't do that and jeopardise all he had. His family and his liberty were far too a higher prize to contemplate going through with that.

After the evening meal was over Priskin decided to act. He rummaged in his jacket for the business card Leonid Chavan had given him, then he retreated into his study. There were several emails waiting in the 'in-box'. One was from the agent for the vendor of the Sussex property. The man who had shown him around the property, thanked him for his communication and acknowledged his bid on behalf of Yuri Asamovich. There was an email from 'Heath and Horner' thanking him for choosing them to represent Mr

Asamovich in the sale of the mansion in Knightsbridge with an asking price of fifty million pounds.

He turned his PC off, sat in the seat and looked at the card for several long moments, then reaching out he took his mobile phone and tapped in the mobile phone number on the card.

The call was answered by a man with a deep Russian accent, though he spoke perfect English. When Priskin responded in Russian then Chavan did likewise. He asked Priskin why he was contacting him.

"I'd like to request a personal meeting with Sergei Molinsky," he replied.

"On what matter?" Chavan asked.

Priskin waited for a moment. "His son-in-law," he said. Chavan didn't ask him why he wanted to discuss Dale Farthing with Molinsky. Perhaps, he already knew he was a loose cannon.

"I will speak to Sergei as soon as possible and get back to you," he said.

Priskin thanked him. No other words were said. He terminated the call.

That evening Priskin took Andre to a local shop to purchase a box of fireworks. It would be the fifth of November in three days.

Olga had invited three of Andre's friends and their parents to the house for a firework party. Hot-dogs and chicken soup were on the menu. His father would oversee the lighting of the fireworks from a safe distance at the bottom of the garden. Olga would make sure Andre was well wrapped up in some warm clothes and that he had a woolly hat on his head, a scarf around his neck and mittens on his hands. Dimitri did think she was a little bit overprotective to their son at times.

Asamovich cancelled the usual Tuesday meeting with Priskin. Rather than meet face-to-face Priskin emailed his boss to update him on the state of play regarding the purchase of the house in Sussex and the sale of his Knightsbridge home.

By Tuesday night, Priskin had still not heard from Leonid Chavan. He was becoming a little anxious about meeting with Molinsky to tell him about Farthing. He still hadn't told Olga about the job offer. If it was genuine, and he had no reason to doubt Molinsky's integrity, then he would say 'yes' he would accept the offer. He did much the same thing for Asamovich, but for half the money Molinsky was offering to pay him. But then he considered that Molinsky might be twice as demanding as Yuri. He might expect him to do three times the amount of work he did for Asamovich. On that score it didn't sound like such a good thing.

It wasn't until Wednesday noon when Priskin received a return call from Leonid Chavan. He kept it short and to the point. Molinsky was happy to see him tomorrow at four in the afternoon. He didn't know why Priskin wanted to talk to him about Dale Farthing. Nevertheless, he agreed to see him. Priskin was invited to visit him in his London home. He had a penthouse apartment in a new residential development close to Battersea Park and overlooking the stretch of the Thames directly opposite Prince Albert Bridge. It was less than a quarter of a mile from his daughter's home. Priskin had to present himself at the security gate at four o'clock precisely. That would give him plenty of time to meet with Molinsky, before returning home to supervise the firework display.

Chapter 23

The apartment block Molinsky resided in was a glass and steel structure, built in a modern style and benefiting from new building methods and materials. After all it was only a year since it opened to residents.

As he approached the building in his car, Priskin had to stop at an iron gate in a steel fence. Security was paramount. The exterior and interior of the building were under constant twenty-four-hour surveillance. He pulled-up by the gate and pressed a button in a communication unit.

He was pensive. He couldn't guess how Molinsky would react when he told him what his son-in-law was up to. He was his daughter's husband. Nevertheless, he thought this was the best way of being able to stop his madness.

A voice came out of the intercom. "Security. What's your business please?" a security operative asked.

"I'm here to meet with Sergei Molinsky," he replied.

"Thank you," said the voice. Priskin was asked to wait for a moment. He was left waiting for another two minutes before a man in a dark security guard uniform came across the yard to slide open the gate and let him drive onto the property. Priskin was asked to park in one of the empty bays by the entrance foyer.

He was met by the uniformed man who escorted him through the locked entrance and into the foyer. At a desk he was asked to sign in. They were certainly taking few chances. The price of an apartment came with a high level of services that included round-the-clock security, twenty-four hours a day, seven days a week, fifty-two weeks of the year.

Molinsky resided in a penthouse apartment on the top floor of the ten-floor building. Priskin took the rapid elevator to the summit. He came out onto a glassed-covered corridor at the rear of the block with a view of Battersea Park fading in colour as the drab light of the day was all but gone at four in the afternoon. There was already an explosion of fireworks in the sky as the Bonfire Night revellers began the festivities early.

There were two penthouse apartments on the tenth floor. Molinsky's was at the end of a long corridor. At the door to the apartment he paused to straighten his tie, then he pressed the doorbell in the frame and waited. Moments later, Leonid Chavan opened the door. He was wearing a pallid jacket, and trousers. He showed Priskin into the apartment.

It was all modern appliances and fittings. Not too dissimilar from the house Asamovich was interested in buying. Chavan led him into a long room. The interior was like a swanky art gallery with high ceilings and a light oak panelled floor.

An assortment of artwork was attached to the walls on three sides. There were Dali type paintings and more contemporary paintings by up-and-coming artist's like Hurvin Anderson, plus works by Modigliani and Magritte. On the other side was a long glass window with a view down to the river several hundred feet below and across to the glass towers in the City and in Canary Wharf. The sharp pointed summit of the Shard on the south bank was just in viewing range.

Chavan opened a pair of double doors that led into a lounge. Sergei Molinsky was sitting on a wide sofa that faced the window. He looked resplendent in a red silk smoking jacket over an opal coloured shirt and dark slacks. The air was free of fragrance. There was no sound except for the faint whistle of wind rushing by the plate-glass window. From this viewpoint the regal and floodlit Albert Bridge looked like a photograph on a tourist postcard.

Molinsky clapped eyes on Priskin and raised a hand. "Dimitri," he said in an ebullient manner. "Welcome to my home," he said in Russian. "What can I do?" he asked. "Something about my son-in-law?"

Priskin remained standing, until Molinsky pointed to a chair set against a pillar. Priskin went to the chair and sat down. Chavan remained in the room.

Priskin took in a deep breath. "I need your advice," he said in Russian.

"What about?" Molinsky asked, instantly reverting to English.

"Dale Farthing is threatening to blackmail Yuri Asamovich," he said straight out.

Molinsky's face didn't change. "What about?" he asked.

Priskin sat back in the chair but didn't cross his legs. "I must admit that I made a stupid error of judgement. I told him about Yuri's possible involvement in the murder of a newspaper journalist back in Moscow in the mid nineteen-nineties. Ninety-five I think. During Yeltsin's middle period."

Molinsky sat up. "And?"

"Dale seems to have got it into his head that Yuri was responsible. Though as I explained to him there is no evidence to link him or anyone else to the murder. Dale doesn't seem to understand this. He said he's going to blackmail Yuri for ten million or else he'll go to the newspapers with the story."

Molinsky sighed. He looked at Chavan for a fleeting moment, then back to Priskin. "For a man who is experienced. He is very silly," he said. "But what can I do?" he asked.

"I was hoping you could speak to him. Ask him to drop it. Now he's threatening me."

"How?" Molinsky asked.

"He's asking me for one million pounds or else he'll inform Asamovich that I told him he ordered the murder."

Molinsky tutted. "My son-in-law is such a fool," he said. "The problem I have got is that he's my daughter's husband. She loves him. I told her he was no good, but she wouldn't listen to me."

Priskin didn't know instantly how to reply. He waited a few moments. "I tried to make it clear to him that Yuri's involvement is only, at best, wild speculation. That whoever ordered the murder didn't pull the trigger. That whoever it was covered their tracks. Then of course there is the embezzlement of the money from the EU fund," he said.

Molinsky pulled himself up off the sofa and stepped to the window. The light from the lamps at each end of the sofa were reflecting in the window. Despite the reflection it was possible to see the lights spread across the city to the north for as far as the eye could see.

Molinsky looked back to look at Priskin. "The only thing I ask is that you don't hurt him," he said. "It would break my daughters heart." He turned back to the window to observe the flashes in the sky. A few long moments passed. As the sky was becoming darker than the flash and sparkle of fireworks were becoming increasingly visible.

Molinsky remained at the window for a further twenty seconds, then he turned and came back to sit on the sofa. "You made a very wise decision to tell me," he said. "Very wise. Leave it with me. I'm going to a business meeting tomorrow. I will ask Dale to accompany me. You can, how the British say, rest assured. You will not hear of this again," he said.

Priskin bowed his head. "Thank you," he said. "I don't want it to go any further. Any help will be greatly appreciated."

Molinsky grinned. "I understand that your wife has become a friend of my daughter," he said.

"That's correct," replied Priskin. "They are two St Petersburg girls," he said, then realised he had plagiarised a line from Farthing.

"Yes. Rightly so," said Molinsky. "Now on that other matter. Have you had chance to consider my offer?" he asked.

"I have," said Priskin.

"What's your decision?" he asked.

"I'm sorry to inform you that I'm going to have to turn it down," said Priskin.

Molinsky pursed his lips. "Is there a reason?" he asked.

"Yuri gave me a job when I was looking for something. I have a certain amount of loyalty to him. He's been very generous to me and my family. I feel it wouldn't be right for me to walk away when he showed faith in me. Therefore, I'm sorry but I must turn your offer down, but thank you for considering me."

"Don't be sorry," said Molinsky. "You're a good man. I like your sense of loyalty to your fellow Russian. I am disappointed, but not hurt by your decision. You've made the right decision to show your loyalty and that is, how the British say, very admirable?"

"Yes, I think that's a good word," Priskin said. Molinsky smiled. "Thank you," he said.

"The invitation to the dinner on Tuesday still stands," said Molinsky. "It will be an excellent evening. His Excellency, the Ambassador for Russia to London will be here. I will be delighted to meet your wife."

"Thank you. We will look forward to it immensely," said Priskin.

Molinsky nodded. "Thank you for speaking to me about this problem with my son in-law. It will be solved," he said. He nodded to Leonid. "Please see our guest out," he asked.

Chavan escorted Priskin out of the room, through the door and back into the hallway, then through the main door and out onto the glass covered landing. The time was half past four. The sky in the distance was dark and grey. A mist, or maybe it was the smoke from burning bonfires thickened the gloom.

Chavan said he would be in touch about the arrangements for the dinner party. Priskin told him he was going to tell his wife to go out and purchase a gown for the evening. If the Russian ambassador was the 'guest of honour' then it was bound to be a night befitting of gowns and tiaras.

Priskin arrived back home for six o'clock. He had one hour to prepare a safe spot at the bottom of the garden for the fireworks.

That evening the Priskin family were joined by three of Andre's school friends and their parents for an evening of fireworks, hot-dogs, and soup. The children were at that age when things that went 'bang' and sparkled, created a great deal of excitement and wonder. Luckily the evening stayed dry, but it was chilly. By eight-thirty the fireworks had all but gone. All that were left were a few sparklers. Everyone, children, and the adults, had had a good time. The hotdogs with lashings of onions and ketchup had gone down well. The children had soft drinks, whilst the adults had beer and wine. By eight-forty it was all over. Andre was wrapped up in bed by nine.

As soon as they were alone Dimitri informed Olga that they had been invited to attend a dinner party at the home of Sergei Molinsky on Tuesday evening. She was delighted. Here was her opportunity to buy that new gown she had seen in a shop on Kensington High Street. This wouldn't be a 'jeans and t-shirt' evening, it would be a night for gowns for the ladies, best suits, silk shirts, and ties for the men.

Things moved quickly on the house selling and buying front. The agent for the seller of the Sussex property was hopeful of securing a deal. 'Heath and Horner' the agents acting for the sale of the Knightsbridge property were confident they would attract a buyer. A nation looking for new premises to relocate their London embassy might be interested in buying the property. One of the senior partners of, 'Heath and Horner' a chap by the name of Darius Weller would be acting for them.

Priskin emailed Asamovich to update him on progress so far. Yuri said he had plans to convert one of the rooms into a jacuzzi and plunge pool. By the time he had finished, the total cost of buying the property, converting two of the rooms and building the storage facility for his cars would probably push the total cost nearer to the nine million pounds mark. He now appeared to be deadly serious about going through with it. It was not looking like one of his projects that would never see the light of day. It would be his sixty-seventh birthday on Tuesday, the tenth.

Chapter 24

The following day, Friday, the smell of gunpower and bonfires was still in the air when Priskin took Andre to school. The more he thought about Asamovich leaving London, then the more he considered getting his family out of the city. There would be plenty of good schools in the Brighton area, plus plenty of affordable homes. The transport links were excellent. London was only an hour and fifteen minutes away on a fast train

By midday there had been significant progress. The agent for the seller of the property in Sussex called Priskin to inform him that the vendor had agreed to the sale at a price of seven million pounds. Priskin then contacted a company called, 'Pascel-Simmington' to carry out a full survey of the property and to look at the feasibility of building a large storage space on the site to house the vintage car collection. His next task was to contact the solicitor acting for Asamovich to instruct them to begin the conveyancing process. All this work was taking his mind off the Dale Farthing affair. He hoped that Molinsky would speak to him and ask him to stop what he was doing. Priskin could only hope Molinsky's persuasion would convince him to drop it.

He had turned down the job with Molinsky not out of a fear of working for Molinsky, but because of his sense of loyalty to Yuri. But also, his desire to close his friendship with Farthing, though his wife was now in Octavia's inner circle of friends.

The partner from, 'Heath and Horner', Darius Weller called him to ask if he could make an appointment to view the property on Knightsbridge to set the ball rolling, so to speak. Priskin agreed to meet him there tomorrow, Saturday, at two in the afternoon.

Darius Weller turned out to be a very nice guy. He was a good-looking tall chap, originally from south London. He came armed with a clip board and a video camera in his briefcase. He took numerous photographs of both the interior and exterior of the house. After a look around the mansion, Priskin took him into the lounge to discuss the terms and conditions, the marketing plan, the cost of putting the house on the market and the rate of commission.

Weller said that he would get back to him with a mock-up of the 'particulars' for the marketing campaign. He said that fifty million pounds was at the top end of the valuation, which seemed to indicate that the asking price was perhaps too much to ask. Nevertheless, he was confident they would attract a buyer and secure the full asking price. Asamovich was not at home that weekend. He was, according to Hector, staying with a lady friend who lived in London. He wouldn't be back home until Wednesday at the earliest. Asamovich and his lady friend would be celebrating his sixty-seventh birthday together on Tuesday.

It was mid-evening on Saturday when Leonid Chavan called Priskin to confirm the details of the dinner party on Tuesday. It would commence at eight o'clock. The men would be expected to wear evening suits, not tuxedos. The ladies should wear gowns. Assuming there wasn't a sudden change in his hectic schedule the ambassador and his wife would attend. As well as the ambassador and his wife, three other couples had been invited. Chavan didn't say who they were.

Priskin was looking forward to the evening. He would be rubbing shoulders with not only Molinsky, but Russia's top man in London. Meeting the ambassador was a big deal. It could open numerous doors for him.

On Sunday, Olga left the house at one o'clock to meet with Octavia Farthing and her friends at the posh bistro in Chelsea for Sunday afternoon drinks, food and chit-chat. Priskin asked her not to mention the dinner party with Sergei Molinsky out of the need to maintain security. She reluctantly agreed.

Chapter 25

Tuesday evening soon came around. A neighbour had agreed to baby sit Andre up to one in the morning. Dimitri and Olga left their home at seven-thirty and took a black-cab to Molinsky's home in the building close to Battersea Park. Priskin was wearing a smart suit he had tailor made from 'Huntsman and Sons' on Savile Row. Olga wore the black shimmering gown she had purchased from the up-market store on Kensington High Street. She looked great. The silver thread around the neck line and around her waist made her look far slimmer than she was. The Gucci hand clasp in her hand was one of her prized possessions. Priskin had given it to her for her thirtieth birthday.

He had not heard from Farthing which lead him to believe that Molinsky had spoken to him and advised him to drop it.

The cabbie dropped them off outside of the gates to the apartment block. It was not too long before they were in the lift going to the top floor. The door to the penthouse was opened by a girl in her early twenties in a maid's uniform. Leonid Chavan soon appeared at the door to greet them and show them inside. Priskin pointed out the fantastic views across the city to Olga. There was a melodic strum of a stringed musical instrument playing inside the apartment.

Chavan opened the second door into the next room. It was the room with all the artwork on the walls. Inside a young dark haired oriental lady in a long white dress was sitting on a stool plucking away on the strings of a golden, full size harp. It made the most exquisite sound possible. In the centre of the room, a large dining table had been erected. It was set with a dozen places, fine silver cutlery was laid out by the sides of name cards, indicating who was sitting where. Flowers in three glazed pots were placed down the centre of the table. The table cloth was whiter than white. The smell of food cooking in the kitchen permeated through the apartment. Two members of a catering team, both in black, were holding a tray of pink champagne in tall, slim flutes. One of them came towards Dimitri and Olga. They helped themselves to a glass.

The door to the lounge came open. Sergei Molinsky and his female partner came into the room followed by Dale and Octavia Farthing. Octavia was wearing a gown that was tucked into her waist and trailed on the floor, so she resembled a mermaid. Dale Farthing was in a silver-blue jacket and pants combination.

Two couples followed the Farthings. Priskin didn't know them. Both the men were stylishly dressed, the ladies were in gowns. Molinsky came forward, smiling. He got inbetween the Priskins and gently took them by the arm. "May I introduce you to Dimitri and Olga Priskin," he said in English. The Priskin's said 'hello' in unison.

Just then the doorbell rang. Chavan went to answer the front door. He returned moments later. Who should step into the room, but Yuri Asamovich with a female partner on his arm.

Priskin was a little stunned. He didn't have a clue that Yuri would be at the party. Molinsky greeted Asamovich like a long-lost friend. They embraced with a full-on, backslapping hug. Priskin had no idea who the lady was. She looked to be in her late forties. Stylish and well maintained. Blonde hair. Slim waist. She was wearing a burgundy-red gown, with a pearl necklace around her neck and matching pearls dangling from her earlobes. She was slightly taller than Asamovich. Priskin looked at him and smiled. Yuri lifted his hand and gave him a wave of recognition. The harpist paused for a moment, before she continued to play. Several members of the catering staff came into the room and began to lay the first course plates at each of the twelve places.

Molinsky raised his hand and asked for silence. "Ladies and gentlemen. It is my good friend Yuri's birthday today." He reached out to take two glasses full of pink champagne, from off one the trays, held by a young man. He handed one each to Yuri and his partner, then he took one himself.

"To Yuri," said Molinsky. He lifted his glass, and everyone did likewise. 'To Yuri' everyone repeated. Now Priskin knew that Molinsky and Asamovich were in fact good friends and acquaintances. Something he had not known in all the time he had worked for Asamovich.

"I have some disappointing news," said Molinsky. "Unfortunately, the Ambassador will not be able to join us this evening. He has urgent business to attend to. There is a Russian trade delegation in London today and they are meeting at the embassy this evening. He sends his apologies. Still, we shall have a good evening. Please be seated," he instructed. "Dinner will be served shortly."

Molinsky was seated at the top of the table. His partner was at the other end, opposite him. She was the same lady Priskin had seen in the hotel the other evening.

Everyone sat at their allocated place. There were twelve people around the table. Priskin was placed with Olga on his right-hand side. He was across the table from a lady he didn't know. The table was now set with bottles of wine in ice-buckets, crystal glasses. The full works.

The chit-chat increased. The aroma of cooking food filled the air. Before the first course was served Molinsky went around the table introducing each guest one-by-one. The people Priskin had never met before were a London based, Russian investment banker and his wife. The other man was an American, by the name of Stephen Landsdorf, and Sylvia, his charming French wife. It was an eclectic mix of people. Priskin still couldn't get over the fact that Asamovich was here. Perhaps, the party was in honour of his sixty-seventh birthday. Which was today.

The door opened and a man in a chef's apron entered the room followed by several waitresses carrying the first course on silver trays. It was so grand, and stage managed. The harpist continued to play.

The first course was a raspberry sorbet in goblet shaped glass bowls. The second course was soup. The main course was Duck l'Orange. A classic French dish served with bigarade sauce, crispy vegetables, and slices of melon. The chef was a Michelin star chef at a top London restaurant. It was fine, lavish dining. Molinsky proposed the first toast to 'friends'. Asamovich proposed the second toast to, 'absent friends'.

Priskin chatted to the lady across the table. She was a pretty red-head, the wife of the American. She spoke with a strong gallic accent that sometimes made her words difficult to understand. Olga was sitting across from her husband who revealed he was from San Francisco, though he now lived in New York City. Priskin had little reason to disbelieve him.

Dale Farthing was sitting on the other side of the table close to Molinsky. He had said very little throughout the first hour. Octavia was chatting to everyone. She had a bubbly personality and an effervescent outlook on life. It was easy to see why she was so popular.

The fourth course was a sweet from a choice of four options. The Priskin's both choose Profiteroles with a fresh cream topping. Priskin was full, but there was still a fifth course to come, followed by coffee and liqueurs.

Chapter 26

By eleven o'clock the party was beginning to wind-down. The flautist had left thirty minutes before. The catering team had cleared away most of the plates and cutlery from the table. The American and his French wife had an early morning flight to New York, so they had departed at ten-forty. The Russian investment banker and his wife left not long after them. There were eight people still at the table. The Priskins. The Farthings. Asamovich and his lady friend. Molinsky and his partner.

Coffee and liqueurs were served at just after eleven o'clock. The chef was introduced to the remaining diners to receive their appreciation for the fine food and the presentation. Molinsky excused himself for a moment. He soon reappeared carrying a small rectangular wooden box that was carved with an intricate, ornate pine design. He asked for silence. Everyone stopped talking and hush descended over the room.

"All of you know today is Yuri's birthday," he said. "I have a small gift for him." He handed the box to Asamovich. Asamovich was taken aback. He got to his feet. He took the box from Asamovich, slid the top open to reveal what was inside. Priskin was stunned.

Two turquoise, gold and silver encrusted Faberge eggs were placed in a silk covered base. They were the two eggs he had bid for on behalf of Asamovich. Molinsky was giving them to Asamovich as a birthday present. The ladies all gasped, not just at the beauty of the eggs, but Sergei's incredible generosity.

Asamovich was nearly overcome with emotion. "My dear Sergei," he said in Russian. "Thank you very much. This is such a lovely surprise and a most beautiful gift. I am honoured by your kindness. I am honoured to be your friend. I will treasure them for the rest of my days," he said. He went to Molinsky, embraced him, and kissed him on both cheeks. It was one of the most moving acts of kinship Priskin had witnessed in a long time.

Immediately after the presentation, Molinsky suggested that the men locate to another room to enjoy a cigar and a glass of vodka. He said he had a box of the finest Montecristo cigars in his study.

The men soon located to the room at the rear of the apartment. It was Molinsky's study. They sat around a dark smoked glass topped table and made themselves comfortable. The room contained a desk, a computer and all the peripheral equipment. A wide screen TV was attached to a wall. A wide window looked out across the dark spread of Battersea Park below.

Molinsky went behind the desk. He opened a drawer and extracted a box of Cuban cigars. He opened the box and passed it around for each of them to take a cigar. Then he clipped the end of his cigar using a cutting tool, which was handed around the room.

Within seconds the room was full of a blue-grey mist from four burning cigars. There was a knock at the door. Leonid Chavan came in, then closed the door behind him. He was carrying a large bottle of vodka and four short glasses which he placed, one, in front of each of the men. He put the bottle down onto the centre of the table next to an ashtray which was already full of ash. He didn't vacate the room, choosing instead to lean against the door.

Molinsky reached out, took the bottle, ripped the seal off, then unscrewed the cap. Then he went around the table topping all four glasses full of the colourless, odourless liquid. When all the glasses were full he took his glass and raised it high. "To Russia," he said.

They each took a glass, lifted it high. "To Russia," they said and each of them knocked the first shot back. Less than ten seconds later Asamovich took the bottle. He filled the four glasses with the second shot. He raised his glass. "To Vladimir Putin," he said.

"To Vladimir Putin," the four of them repeated, took their glass, tipped it back and emptied the contents down their throats.

Molinsky looked to Yuri Asamovich. "My dear Yuri. You and I have been through a great deal," he said. "We go back a long way. All the way back to the nineteen-eighties in our homeland when we both worked for the KGB," he said. This was a revelation Priskin had not expected. "For the record I want to admit that we both took from that European Fund. We were not the only ones to do so. So, on that account it did what it was designed for," he said. His face didn't crack into a smile. He didn't chuckle. He was being deadly serious.

Asamovich took the cigar from out his mouth. He nodded his head. "That is true my dear friend," he said. Just then there was a knock at the door. Chavan opened it. A sixth man entered the room. Priskin could hardly see through the mist swirling through the room. It took him a moment to see it was one of Molinsky's bodyguards.

Molinsky turned to greet him. "This is Alexi. He worked for me in Moscow. When we had the problem with that newspaper reporter we did what we had to do. Alexi eliminated him on our orders," he said. Then as if the word 'orders' was a code word Alexi undid the button holding his jacket closed across his chest. He pulled the flap back to reveal the dark object in the leather strap holster under his left side armpit. It was a black shinny handgun. Priskin felt a jolt go through his bones. With the four ladies in the room down the corridor it was highly unlikely that Alexi would withdraw the weapon and start shooting, but it was still an ominous development.

Molinsky coughed lightly. "We agreed to kill the journalist to stop him from talking and revealing who had taken from the fund. Now you both know," he said, first looking at his son-in-law then at Priskin. "We'll do it again if we have to," he added.

"If we must," added Asamovich in a cold, chilling tone of voice. Alexi closed his jacket over his rock-hard stomach. It was like a scene from some Shakespeare drama or a gangster movie, thought Priskin. It was a warning to both Farthing and to him not say a word of this.

"Do you understand?" Molinsky asked. Priskin nodded his head. Farthing did likewise.

Molinsky reached out to the centre of the table to grasp the bottle of vodka. Chavan opened the door. Both he and Alexi stepped out. Chavan closed the door behind him.

Molinsky looked at Farthing. "Your turn to fill the glasses and give a toast," he said.

Before Farthing could take hold of the bottle, Molinsky reached out and grasped the bottle from him. "I'll propose the next toast," he said. He poured four more shots into the four glasses. In his haste some of the liquid spilled onto the table. He took his glass and lifted it high. He paused for a moment to think of an appropriate toast. "To loyalty," he said in a booming voice. He nodded his head towards Priskin, but then turned to look at his son-in-law and gave him the dirtiest most meaningful scowl possible. It was the scowl of a man who had just issued the most fearsome warning, but without having to utter a word. Farthing looked incredibly sheepish as if he knew the message in the toast was directed at him. He had just been well and truly admonished.

He, Priskin and Asamovich took their glasses. "To loyalty," they said in unison. All four of them downed the third shot. There was no need for handshakes or anything like that. This was like a 'breaking of bread'. Instead of bread, Russians did it with vodka.

Priskin was asked to fill the glasses and propose the fourth and final toast. He did so. "To friendship," was his toast.

"To friendship," the other three repeated.

As soon as the glasses were empty, and the toasts had been given, Molinsky suggested they re-join the ladies in the other room. Priskin felt a little shaky on his legs but managed to get up. The four men left the study with the cigars still in their hands and returned to the room where the ladies were sitting at the dining table drinking fine wine from silver goblets. Octavia was telling another one of her funny stories.

Before joining his wife Priskin took a moment to look out of the window at the twinkling lights spread across the city. At this time of the night the view was stunning. Far away into the distance the arch of the top of the London Eye was just visible. The time was fast approaching midnight.

After a minute, Molinsky turned the internal lights out and asked everyone to join him at the window. The ladies got up from the table and everyone joined the host at the window to look out across the city. Free from the glare of internal light the city had never looked finer, but of course it didn't compare with the beauty of St Petersburg, or for that matter, Moscow. They all agreed on that.

THE END

33265661R00129

Printed in Poland
by Amazon Fulfillment
Poland Sp. z o.o., Wrocław